SEARCH IN THE DESERT

FRANKLIN FOLSOM

Search in the Desert

DECORATIONS BY
MARY AND STANLEY HIGHSMITH

Funk & Wagnalls Company New York
1957

Library of Congress Catalog Card Number 55–11098
Printed in the United States of America

2

To my son Michael

SEARCH IN THE DESERT

Chapter 1

Joe enjoyed the nip in the April air as he tuned up his father's truck. Once in a while he stood away from the throbbing engine, stretched for a minute, and looked around the old place. It was good to be back here, close to the mountains on the ranch where he'd grown up.

In the past three years he'd made only a few flying trips to see his folks. Maybe this time he'd stick around for a month or so at least. He could tinker with the machinery and lend a hand at the general work. With luck it would be a busy season for his father, who ran the small ranch as a feeder lot where he fattened cattle for the market.

Joe's head was under the hood of the truck when a new Cadillac turned off the road and came up the long muddy driveway toward the house. He didn't even hear the car pull into the yard. But the sound of whistling brought him to with a start. He'd know that signal anywhere, even though it had been a long time since he'd heard it. Two short loud whistles, then two more, had been the private signal system that he and Perry Burns had used when they were in high school.

Joe whirled around. It was Perry all right, and with him, getting out of the other side of the car, was Perry's father, Andrew Burns. If the President himself had driven thirty miles out from Denver to call on him, Joe wouldn't have been more surprised. It wasn't remotely in the natural order of things for Mr. Burns, head of the Colorado and Western Mining Company, to drive the three miles from Boulder to see Joe Fraser. In all the years when Perry had biked out to the ranch every week—sometimes every day after school—Mr. Burns himself had never come.

"Well, hello!" Joe called in open astonishment. He stepped away from the truck, wiped his hands on a rag, and swung his long legs quickly across the yard toward his visitors.

"Hi, you old rock hound." He gave Perry a resounding whack on the shoulder. "Where you been hiding?" In the old days Perry had made the ranch a second home, but things had changed. Life had pulled the two of them in different directions. Joe had been away, and as for Perry, Joe summed it up when he added, "I'd begun to think you'd never get your nose out of a book."

"Hoped we'd find you here," Mr. Burns said, turning on a smile. "We heard you were back."

"We tried to get you on the phone, but there was no answer, so we took a run out," Perry added. But the explanation didn't clear up very much in Joe's mind.

"Didn't hear it ring, and there's nobody else home. Family's in town shopping," Joe said. "What's new?"

"I'm taking Perry out of college—until next fall anyway," Mr. Burns answered. "Sending him into the field to get some practical experience uranium prospecting. Do him good, and he's piled up so many extra credits he could almost graduate now. But that can wait—and uranium can't. I need every man I can get in the field. So Perry is going to make himself useful."

The papers had been full of the uranium boom, but Joe hadn't paid much attention. Long ago, during the First World War, his uncle had tried prospecting and had gone broke looking for tungsten, which was the rage then. For every prospector who struck it rich, a hundred or a thousand lost everything they had. No, thank you. Joe wanted excitement, sure, but he'd figured out a way to have it—plus a paycheck every week. He'd gone off to learn helicoptering on the GI bill after he got back from Korea. Copters were the coming thing.

It was different with Perry. His grubstake was guaranteed even if he didn't make a strike. He ought to enjoy this racket.

"Lucky stiff." Joe grinned down amiably at Perry, who was a good four inches shorter than his five feet eleven. "But a prospector has to eat. You'll be committing suicide if you don't learn to cook better biscuits than you used to."

Perry's placid face broke into a self-conscious smile. He was used to Joe's ribbing. Many a week-end when they were kids they had strapped blankets and grub onto their pack boards and hiked up into the Colorado mountains west of Boulder. Together they had climbed to the top of nearly every high point, from the green foothills way back to the austere peaks on the Continental Divide.

"Perry's got a stomach of iron," Mr. Burns boasted, trying to get into the act. "What I'm worried about is yours, Joe. Can you eat your own biscuits?"

"I keep my hatchet sharp to crack 'em open. Nothing to it after that—my teeth are good," Joe assured him. "But I don't need 'em here at home. My mother bakes a biscuit—" he nudged Perry ostentatiously, "like a soft morning cloud, and the honey and butter run off it like sunlight in June." Then: "Know anybody who wants to hire a jim-dandy copter pilot?"

"I like a man who comes to the point," Mr. Burns said approvingly. What the point was, Joe could only guess, but

Burns went on. "Do you mind showing me your pilot's license?"

Now the old boy was getting down to cases, Joe thought. "Come into the house where it's warmer, while I dig it out," he suggested.

Mr. Burns looked curiously around the living-room as Joe led him in, and Joe had never felt more acutely aware of the difference between the linoleum carpet under his feet and the Persian rugs he'd walked on so many times in the Burns living-room.

Mr Burns studied the crisp new diploma from the Ajax Aviation School, Teterboro, New Jersey. Then Joe handed him his license.

"Helicopters are so new," he explained, "you don't get a special license. You just get a copter rating on a pilot's ticket. That means I can fly both a copter and a private plane." There was also a to-whom-it-may-concern letter vouching for Joe's good character and stating that he was a qualified aviation mechanic as well as a pilot.

"Speed is the big thing in this uranium game," Mr. Burns said impressively. "Some of my geologists are using planes and getting good results from the air. But I've been looking into the matter and I think there is a place for helicopters in the field. Not so much to do aerial prospecting but to reach tough places in a hurry. Planes usually can't land within miles of a spot where they've located signs of radioactivity." Then he added suddenly, "What do you think about using copters in the Four Corners area?"

Joe was surprised to have his opinion sought. Burns wasn't the kind of man to ask advice from a younger person.

"Nothing like a copter to go where nothing else can," Joe said, and he meant it. "All you need is a flat place about forty by forty, or even less, and you can set one of these babies down. Of course, you've got to stay fairly near a supply of gas. And if it's high altitude you want, you'd better forget a copter in hot weather out in this country. Otherwise there's nothing to beat them. And they're a lot safer than planes."

"What kind of copter would you recommend?"

"You mean just for taxiing a prospector or two into the field?"

"That's right."

"A Bell would be good if you don't have heavy equipment."

"You seem to know your business," Burns said bluntly. "That's just what I've concluded, and I can get one delivered next week. Do you want to fly it for me? I always try to give jobs to local boys when I can."

"Would I like to!" Joe had only been home from school a couple of weeks for a visit. Now a job had walked up and asked him to take it. "When do I start?" What a break! He'd be camping out with Perry again—it couldn't be better.

"Will sixty a week and board and room be satisfactory?"

This was low pay for a pilot, Joe knew, and he'd do the work of a mechanic as well, but who cared about money? He'd see new country. Get experience. *And* take in a mining boom.

"Whatever you say is all right with me." Joe was more casual than he felt. Then he had a sudden misgiving. "You really serious?" he asked.

"Absolutely," Mr. Burns assured him. "Naturally I wouldn't let you go off in an expensive thing like a copter—I'm putting fifteen thousand into it—unless I felt sure you were responsible. I don't want the machine cracked up, and

I don't want anything to happen to Perry. I'm putting a lot of trust in you, but from what I've seen, I'm making a safe bet."

The flattery in the words was pleasant, but also somehow irritating, almost insulting. The old buzzard thinks about his machine first, then about his kid.

"And one more thing," Mr. Burns added with an air of expansive geniality. "Just for the record, it's naturally understood with all our employees in the field that if any of them should happen to strike uranium while they're on the payroll, the company has sole right to the claim. The same rule applies to any claim in the area that's filed within a year by a former employee. I'm sure you'll agree this is fair. Men in the field can catch uranium fever and do unethical things. We've found it saves a lot of hard feelings if every employee, without distinction, signs an agreement along these lines. My lawyer will send it to you."

The old boy trusts me with his son and his copter—but not with uranium that isn't even his yet. . . . Joe smiled, but all he said was, "Sure. That's OK with me. I'm a pilot, period. . . . You going to grow a prospector's beard, Perry?"

"What's the best way to get the copter down to Cortez?" Mr. Burns went on.

"Ship it by truck."

"You and Perry will make your base of operations in Cortez. My friend, Arnold Spencer, will put you up at his ranch near there whenever you're not out in the field. He's got a landing strip for his own plane, so I can fly down easily if anything turns up. You'll get gas and supplies from him."

Perry, who had let his father do all the talking, now

went out to his car and brought back some maps. On them he pointed out the area he intended to prospect. It lay along the eastern side and the top of the Chuska range of mountains on the Arizona-New Mexico line just south of the Four Corners—the spot where those states and Colorado and Utah all meet.

"That's in the Navaho Reservation," Joe noticed. "What about the Indians? Will they let you prospect on their land?"

"That's the least of our troubles," Mr. Burns laughed. "I've got permission to prospect on the Chuskas south of where a mine has already opened up. You'll see plenty of Indians all right, but they're not likely to bother you. Don't worry about the Navahos. We'll take care of them."

Joe wasn't worried about the Navahos, but he found, as the job became a fact, that he was curious about them. He'd never actually seen an Indian except at rodeos in Boulder and Cheyenne where a few Sioux danced in buckskin costumes.

While Perry and his father arranged for delivery of the copter and bought what seemed to be a whole laboratory full of scientific equipment, Joe cooled his heels.

But one day late in April Perry met him in Denver, and they rummaged through Army and Navy stores for rucksacks, blankets, and other outing equipment. As the two of them pawed over a counter full of canteens of assorted sizes and shapes, Joe felt a twinge of nostalgia. Such intense hours of planning and shopping had been an essential part of their boyhood hikes.

But the spell broke quickly as they looked at house trailers. Perry finally settled for a sleek aluminum job that was a gadgeteers delight—and Joe enthusiastically approved of it. Living in this tiny apartment-on-wheels would be prospecting de-luxe.

However, it would in no way resemble Joe's romanticized memories of sleeping under the stars and talking over the problems of life and eternity to the staccato accompaniment of burning pine logs.

Joe fretted as he waited for Perry to iron out every detail of the arrangements. He sensed that there were more differences than merely the fancy gear between this expedition and their boyhood adventures. The two of them had seen very little of each other after Perry went on to college and Joe took a job in a garage in Denver. Then came the two years in the Army. By the time Joe came back to Boulder, Perry was all wrapped up in mineralogy. He had no time for hikes, or dances, or even for a friendly coke now and then. Perry had changed. There was very little he and Joe had to talk about.

Joe waited restlessly for the day when he would head for the Spencer ranch. Funny thing—he'd never been to the southwest part of his own state. The four-hundred-and-seventy-mile drive to Cortez would be an adventure in itself.

CHAPTER 2

An odd-looking figure caught Joe's eye as he drove up to the collection of buildings on the Spencer ranch. Near the corral a dark-skinned young man in a big cowboy hat was unsaddling a horse. The hat was black, and its stiff brim stuck straight out all the way around. Something else made it different from the usual cowboy Stetson—the top, instead of being creased or dented or flattened, rose into a high dome, just the way it must have come from the factory. A small bun of hair, like a woman's, hung down below it at the nape of the neck. An Indian . . .

Loping over the grass in front of the ranch house, Perry called out a welcome, and Joe grinned with mixed affection and amusement at the sight of him. Perry's legs always seemed to trail behind his body—as if his head was determined to get somewhere, whether his feet did or not.

"Hi! I was beginning to worry," Perry said. "You're late. Have trouble on the road?"

"No trouble, but this jeep is straight from the factory and I had to take it easy while I was breaking it in."

"Did the trailer follow all right on the curves?" Perry wanted to know.

"Sure thing, and it's light as a feather. Had to keep looking back to make sure I hadn't left it somewhere."

"Come on in. You've got time to wash before supper."

Joe had stayed in hotel rooms a few times when he'd had week-end passes in the army, but the room to which Perry had led him beat anything he'd ever seen in a hotel. Blond modern furniture, including a kind of chaise-longue affair. It even had a private bath.

He wasn't sure what to wear for supper in such a swank set-up. Not that he had much choice. He hadn't figured on anything so fancy when Mr. Burns mentioned a ranch, and he'd only brought along levis and work shirts, plus a pair of half-way decent slacks and some sport shirts. He settled for the slacks and a sport shirt and went downstairs.

Perry stood talking to Arnold Spencer—the husky, hearty, middle-aged rancher, who was in levis. Two girls in the big living-room wore levis, too. Perry introduced the short, dark one as Pat, Mr. Spencer's daughter. The other girl—as tall as Joe—was Helen-May, a classmate from Pat's prep school in Texas.

A raucous clang sounded outside the house. Someone was beating an old-fashioned iron triangle to summon all hands for a meal. The call postponed any conversation. And there was scarcely a word said at the table, even when a chubby, jovial-looking little man trotted in late and was introduced as Buss Gillmore, "from Washington." Silence at meals, like the banging of the triangle and the ubiquitous blue jeans, was a hangover from early ranch days. When old-time cowboys gathered to eat, they were ravenous from long hours in the saddle, and conversation only stood between them and their primal need for food. Arnold Spencer still ate with traditional singleness of purpose, and Joe guessed he showed the same energy and decision in everything else he did.

The only sound at the table, beside the occasional clink of

knife and fork on plate, was the rustle of two middle-aged Mexican women as they brought in large second-helpings of beefsteak and fried potatoes. Seeing them reminded Joe of the Indian. At least one old ranch custom wasn't honored here as tenaciously as the habit of silent meals. Time was when the hands on a ranch ate at the table with the family. The Indian and any cowboys around this place obviously had their meals somewhere else. Joe guessed he himself wouldn't be at the table if he hadn't been Perry's friend.

When he had finished his apple pie and coffee, Joe followed Perry and the two girls out of the dining-room onto the wide, screened-in porch. There ought to be a way of organizing up a little fun here.

Pat at least seemed willing to be sociable. "When's your heeliocopter coming?" she asked. "I'm just dying to see it. Will you give us a ride in it?"

"I'll be glad to give you a ride, if it's all right with Perry here," Joe said gallantly, answering the second question first. "But," he added with mock sternness, "there's one thing I have to warn you about. Every copter pilot knows it's bad luck, sometimes it's even fatal, to take up a passenger who mispronounces the name for this wonderful new blessing to earthbound mortals. I make it an absolute rule never to fly a passenger unless he—or she—calls a whirlybird a *heli*-copter. H-e-l as in Helen."

"H-e-l as in Helen. That's easy to remember," Pat said. "Helicopter, helicopter, helicopter. You pronounce it right, Helen-May, so we can both go."

"Helicopter." Helen-May managed the word, giving it a special high-pitched Texan sound. She had sat down as soon as they reached the porch, probably to hide the fact that she was so tall.

"Perry dear, you'll let us go up won't you?" Pat stood on her tip-toes as she pleaded.

"I'm sure we can arrange it," Perry answered, looking thoroughly uncomfortable—not so much, Joe guessed, at having to promise the use of the copter, as at the silly chatter and at Pat's flirtatiousness. "Please excuse me," he added. "There's some work I've got to do."

The girls too excused themselves. They had to dress for a party in Durango about forty miles away.

Mr. Spencer, in the living-room, had been laughing at

jokes that Gillmore told. Now they were seriously discussing something called the Bureau of Indian Affairs, which they both seemed to regard as an irritating rash on the body politic. This didn't interest Joe, and anyway he didn't know how to break into the company of the two older men. So he decided to turn in early.

Next morning the entire Spencer household drifted out to stare at the copter, resting lightly on the semi-trailer that delivered it. With its plexiglass-covered cockpit and long slender tail, it resembled—according to Pat—a huge, wingless dragon fly. The big rotor blades and the little tail rotor, too, had been removed and crated for the trip.

After the truck driver and his helper and Joe had expertly winched the machine down skids and onto the ground, Arnold Spencer took charge. He piloted his own Navion and felt quite able to answer questions about any aircraft.

Joe, itching to make sure the copter had arrived in good shape, was glad Spencer liked to be the center of attention. Let him answer the questions.

When Spencer's interest died down, he shooed Pat, Helen-May, Buss Gillmore, and even Perry into the house. The two Mexican women who had watched proceedings from the kitchen door quietly disappeared. No one was around at all now—except the Indian whom Joe had seen the day before. He was tinkering with a bridle near the barn.

"Joe," Spencer called from the front porch. "If you need any help with those rotors call on Manny. He's over there by the stable, and don't let him pretend he doesn't understand English, because he does."

Joe looked at the young fellow Spencer called Manny. His slender figure was just disappearing into the barn. Joe would need help all right with the long rotor blades, but he wasn't sure what kind of assistance this Indian would give. He headed for the barn. "My name's Joe," he said. The Indian stood, his back to him, hanging a bridle on the rough board wall. Now he turned, and Joe saw a handsome broad face under the black hat. The features were expressionless, and the black eyes shifted instantly away from Joe to the open doorway through which he had come.

"I'm Joe Fraser." He held out his hand, and when the Indian took it, Joe had never felt such a limp, lifeless grip.

"I've got a two-man job to do on that machine. Could you knock off a while and hold some things for me? I'd appreciate it a lot. Mr. Spencer said it would be all right."

"I heard him." The words had an edge to them. "You want me now?"

"Whenever you're ready, but if you're busy maybe I can look up one of the other guys around the place."

"I'm the only one here right now. The others are moving steers up onto the range."

"You must have finished the spring round-up early." Joe knew the cycle of ranch life—farther north, at least. "How many head do you run?"

"The white fellows punch cattle. I just wrangle Spencer's own string." This was stated as a simple matter of fact, but it was plain that Manny knew horse-wrangling was the lowliest job on a ranch.

Joe needed willing cooperation. If this Manny was a sore-head, he could louse up the copter but good. But before Joe could think of anything to say, Manny stepped out of the barn and into a nearby shed. He came back with a hammer and wrecking bar. . . . The guy was no dope. He knew what had to be done first.

"You have all the other tools you need?" Manny asked. "Spencer's got everything here for his Navion."

Joe had everything—he hoped. Old man Burns said he'd ordered all the tools and spare parts shipped with the copter.

After the rotors were uncrated and the tool box opened, Joe stood up for a breather and reached into his pocket for cigarettes. He shook one loose in the pack and offered it to Manny. There seemed to be a flicker of hesitation in Manny's eyes, but the Indian accepted the cigarette and a light.

"You come from around here?" Joe asked. He was full of curiosity, but he didn't know where to begin asking questions.

"Reservation. Navaho Reservation."

A part of the Ute Reservation lay nearby. So Manny was a Navaho, not a Ute.

"I didn't know Indians lived away from reservations. You worked here long?" Joe was afraid his ignorance might offend Manny, but he really was curious.

"We work off the reservation—when we can." Manny replied. "There's no law against it. Been here a month."

By mid-afternoon they had the copter assembled. Manny had worked the whole time—often seeing what had to be done before Joe spoke, and always moving with a kind of fluid ease.

"You sure know your way around machinery," Joe said. "Where'd you learn it? School?"

"Some in school. Some in the Army."

"You a GI too?" Joe looked unconsciously at the bundle of hair hanging on Manny's neck. That was no GI haircut.

"Got out about eighteen months ago," Manny replied. Joe looked again at the hair. Maybe it could grow that much in eighteen months. The knot wasn't very big.

"What was your outfit?"

Manny mentioned a division that Joe knew had been in Korea.

"We must have been in Korea at the same time. Well, what d'ya know! It's a small world, as the feller says."

This called for another smoke, and again Joe offered a cigarette. Manny declined this time and seemed to withdraw into himself. But as Joe took his own cigarette, Manny reached silently for the pack, helped himself, returned the pack, then stood for some time just holding the cigarette crosswise between his right thumb and forefinger.

Joe watched with interest, guessing that Manny was trying to decide whether or not to say something.

"This is the way a Navaho holds a cigarette when he gives it to you," he finally said.

Joe had a feeling Manny wanted to make a point of some sort, but he wasn't sure what it was. Experimentally he took a cigarette and offered it, holding it crosswise. "This the way?" he asked.

Manny grunted in the affirmative, and a shy grin passed over his handsome features.

"What's the pitch?" Joe felt encouraged to ask.

"Pointing anything at a Navaho—a cigarette, or a stick, or a finger—is just like thumbing your nose at a white man."

Joe was flabbergasted.

In the days that followed, Joe filled in some of his vacant hours talking with Manny, who was always reticent, but usually willing to say at least something. Only once did he hang an impenetrable curtain of silence around himself. That was when Joe talked enthusiastically about the uranium prospecting that lay ahead of him in the Chuskas.

Drawn by the magnet of their common experience, they touched often in their halting conversations on army life.

"How did you like it?" Joe asked once as Manny was currying Spencer's Arabian mare.

"The way a sheep likes to be dipped."

Joe knew that sheep hated being driven through troughs filled with foul-smelling liquid in which they had to be soaked to prevent scabies. But he also knew that dipping was good for them. Was that what Manny meant? Joe himself hadn't liked army life. His sergeant was a heel. His captain was a stuffed shirt. He couldn't see much sense to the war. But worst of all he had been endlessly bored.

"How come?" Joe asked.

"They kept putting me in the guard house."

"Awol, or something like that?" Joe knew white soldiers who were constantly in trouble because they couldn't fit themselves into the inflexible compartments of army life. Somehow he couldn't imagine this guy marching. Manny had none of the angular, precise motions demanded by the sergeant's "Hup, two, three, four." Every motion he made seemed to flow like water in a stream bed.

"I got the guard house once for taking on too much of that Japanese saki, but that wasn't the big trouble. Three different times when I was off on a pass I got arrested as a Chinese spy. I finally quit asking for passes."

That was one gripe Joe had never heard. For the first time he realized there was a kind of Chinese look to Manny. His big cowboy hat kept you from noticing the way his eyes slanted just a little. Manny's complexion was a little darker than the few Chinese PW's he'd seen. But no question about it. Some slap-happy MP might think he was a Chinese disguised as a GI. And the way he talked wouldn't help, either. He spoke good English, but his words sounded as if they were packed around with soft cotton. He didn't talk like other GIs who'd been born speaking English. Maybe you could mistake him for a Chinese who had learned English in school.

The copter was ready to fly on the second day, ready and tested. It was a good machine, all set to do the hard work for Perry that burros had done for earlier generations of prospectors. The thought of the little beasts of burden gave Joe an inspiration. Burros had achieved distinction in the West as "Rocky Mountain canaries," because of the appalling, brassy brays they let loose on the defenseless wilderness. Now, the sturdy little copter was not only going to do their chores, but she also made a terrible racket. Rocky Mountain Canary would be her name. No, that was too much. He'd call her the Canary for short—and the Canary she became.

Now, what was Perry waiting for? To Joe a uranium rush should be a rush. Load some grub into the trailer. Haul it up to wherever their camp was to be. Come back in the jeep so Joe could get the copter. Then go back to the camp with both the copter and the jeep—and get out into the field.

But it wasn't that simple for Perry. He checked and double-checked supplies. He pored over maps to make sure just where to put his camp, and he drove off on trips to look over the terrain and to talk with other mining men in his father's company. He checked the equipment in his room, which he'd turned into an assayer's office and mineralogist's laboratory. Days went by, and Joe had nothing to do but keep testing the copter.

In a way this was a good thing, he had to admit. The air up near great mountains and buttes—and even over the wide flatlands—didn't feel at all the way the air did back at sea level where he'd learned to fly.

The delay also gave time for the rides that Pat and Helen-May kept begging. He took the two of them up several times—although after the first trip he swore a great private oath he'd never do it again. Pat, who sat next to him, had grabbed his right arm in such terror when he took off that he nearly lost control. He came within a split second of having a first-rate crack-up only a couple of hundred feet from the Spencer ranch house.

"Leggo, you idiot!" he had roared with mixed anger and fear, and it was only when they were safely in the air that he calmed down and looked at the two girls. Helen-May hadn't twittered in her high-pitched voice—or at least Joe hadn't noticed it under the roar of the engine and the rotor. She was calmly looking ahead and down through the plexiglass bubble that surrounded them. Then she looked out on the right side where she sat, and up—at the sky where only a few clouds floated. She seemed mildly interested in the fact that you could get a much better view from a copter than from a plane.

But Pat had turned pale. She shifted away from Joe and stared off to the right at nothing. After they passed beyond the spring green of her father's large pastures, she seemed to get the feel of the copter and edged over toward Joe again.

"You shouldn't have called me an idiot," she yelled. "Gentlemen aren't supposed to say things like that to ladies."

Pat had come so near to wrecking the helicopter that Joe

thought he had shown remarkable self-control. "Ladies shouldn't grab the pilot's arm either."

"The take-off was so different from Daddy's plane, I got scared. I won't again."

Pat sat quietly for the next twenty minutes, until Joe brought the copter down. It was the same on the other short rides he gave the girls. He thought once or twice of asking Pat to go to the movies with him. But that meant he'd have to take Helen-May, too, and she was more than he could stand. Perry wouldn't be a sport and come along to keep Helen-May company. He said he had too much work to do. Perry was busy, the girls were always going off someplace to visit Pat's friends—and Joe kept on fretting.

Then Perry finally announced they'd start into the field the next day. Wishing there was something at least he could do on the copter, Joe ambled out toward the stables.

"Want to go up?" he said to Manny. "Spencer's in Cortez with the girls."

Shy though he was, Manny didn't try to conceal his surprise—or his eagerness. In the air he sat as far forward as he could in his safety belt and looked as if he was making a tremendous discovery about the world. But once the discovery was made, he concentrated on the instrument panel and on Joe's steady pressure on the two control sticks. Here was a guy who wanted to learn to fly, Joe thought. Maybe there would be a chance to teach him before the summer was over.

But the time wasn't now. Next morning the expedition into the Chuskas began.

Chapter 3

Joe's muscular arms were tense with the effort of holding the two vibrating control sticks. The Canary was a good little machine, but Perry, who sat beside him and gave the orders, had demanded too much.

"Can't get any more altitude," Joe shouted above the roar of the engine and rotor blades.

A quick calculation showed 8200 feet above sea level and 1950 feet above the flats which lay to the east of the Chuska mountains. The machine was supposed to be good for 11,000 feet. That would be well above the highest point in the Chuskas.

"Give it another try," Perry insisted, and he looked stubbornly through the plexiglass at the steep, forested slopes and red cliffs ahead.

"Sun's too high. Air's thinned out already," Joe protested.

All this week they'd been flying out of their field camp sixty-five miles south and west of Cortez. Joe had tried everything in the books to get the Canary up as high as Perry wanted to go. He had jockeyed around in search of rising air currents that could help lift him onto the plateau stretching for miles along the top of the Chuskas. But in seven days of trying, he'd never once made it. Instead, he'd been forced to settle down on a kind of giant stair-step that broke the eastern slope of the mountain nearly a thousand feet below his objective.

The search for the elusive currents which might help him had given Joe some bad moments. Several times the copter had dropped right out from under him in a down-draft. In the air that eddied and swirled, sucked down and heaved up, close by the mountains, active, enormous forces attacked the little machine without warning.

Perry always seemed unaware of the danger, and Joe hadn't made any point of telling him. The moments of fear —and exhileration—which came to him during this running battle against the rare, dry atmosphere were his own private affair. He liked the idea of pioneering with a whirlybird in the Four Corners area, and a stubborn streak in him was offended by the limitation of his machine.

But a fact was a fact. Joe had to admit to himself that a service ceiling of 11,000 feet meant one thing in cool, moist air and something else again in this arid, sun-baked country.

"Sun's too high. Air's thinned out," Joe repeated firmly. There came a point beyond which he didn't have to take orders from Perry, even though Perry was the boss.

Joe held his altitude and turned away from the mountain so he could get a better view of possible landing places. The rim that marked the beginning of the high, flat top was tantalizingly obvious. Few, if any, white men had ever explored the tableland beyond that rim. Only one road crossed over it to Lukachukai down on the western side—anyway, only one road that cars could negotiate. But Spencer, who had flown over all these mountains in his Navion, said there were many open parks in the forest. Joe could land the copter in any of them—if he could get that high.

Below him now were slopes covered with pinyon and juni-

per, which rose sharply from the barren plain. Ahead, an intermittent band of cliffs burst through stands of ponderosa pine. The best Joe could do was land on one of those cliff tops, just as he'd been doing every day for a week.

"You'll have to hike again," he bellowed at Perry and turned back toward the face of the escarpment. Perry shrugged his annoyance, then pointed at a section of the cliff they had not yet tried.

Joe studied it and the contours of the slope on either side. The rock was perpendicular and high. There seemed to be no canyons close by to funnel away the air in an unpredictable current. Even if the temperature went a good deal higher by the end of the day, he could literally fall off the cliff, and the whirling rotor would break the drop of the machine. Of course, if the tail rotor or the tip of a blade didn't quite clear the rocks, it would be curtains. But by now he felt he had mastered the trick. He was sure he could make it.

Joe drew in closer to the mountain studying everything ahead and below. "Hey, look!" he shouted. "There's one of those things the Navahos live in."

"A *hogan,*" Perry said a little pedantically, scarcely looking down at the dome-shaped roof of mud which covered the hexagonal log building.

On sudden impulse, Joe maneuvered toward the hogan, then dropped gently down and hovered to get a closer look. In the week he'd been flying over the northeast corner of the Navaho Reservation, he had not yet been close to one of the small windowless huts in which the Indians lived.

A woman rose hastily from a small outdoor fire. Her flowing green skirt made a bright bit of color against the drab earth as she ran toward the door, dragging two little children with her. At the edge of the clearing around the hogan a horse kicked up dust. A boy in the saddle yanked on the reins.

Joe still hovered, taking in the scene. He realized too late that the copter had scared the horse. It reared, lunged frantically, tossed the boy from its back, and then dashed away into the timber.

"Free rodeo," Joe shouted, trying to cover with a smart crack the embarrassment he felt at the trouble he'd caused. Perry shrugged again. The Canary sped away over the treetops and regained the lost altitude. Soon she was high enough to swoop down toward the cliff top.

Joe wanted to land on the very edge of the precipice, facing the emptiness beyond. Near the end of the glide—just when it seemed he would hurtle on past the bare stretch of rock that was his target—he put firm pressure on both control sticks. The Canary responded like a reined-in quarter horse. She leaned back on her haunches, hesitated, then settled gently with the tips of the skids only four feet from the edge of the cliff.

Perfect, Joe thought with satisfaction, as he cut off the engine and waited for the rotor to quit swinging and for the dust cloud it stirred up to settle. Nothing wrong with this buggy that a supercharger couldn't fix, he thought. With a supercharger the engine could get enough oxygen to handle any reasonable altitude. Some company would probably come out with one about the time he finished this job. Be just his luck.

Perry had already stepped down from the cockpit, and was coughing and sneezing in the dust, as he assembled his equipment—Geiger counter, rock hammer, notebook, canteen, and lunch.

"Looks like we'll have to give up any idea of landing on the plateau," Perry said, and there was just a note in his voice that made Joe feel that Perry blamed him. Joe didn't like it. But what Perry said next, after he had strapped on all his gear, sounded a little better. "We'll have to see if the jeep can get around on top of the mountain. Anyway, the copter is saving a lot of time along here. . . . I'll work north," he added, then started off. As an experienced mountaineer he always left word about the direction he planned to take. In case anything happened to him, Joe would know where to look.

All this had been routine every day since they came into the field. Joe taxied Perry to some difficult spot early in the morning. Then he waited all day while Perry walked slowly over the surrounding area, probing with his Geiger counter at each outcrop of rock. Usually Joe killed some of the time greasing the Canary's bearings. The gritty dust he stirred up every time he landed or took off would play havoc with the bearings if he wasn't careful.

But there was no hurry about the grease job. Joe felt vaguely annoyed with the Canary for selling him short on altitude. He didn't like Perry's constant pressure to get up higher either. Anyway, it was only eight o'clock now, and they wouldn't start the return trip until five-thirty or so in the afternoon. Uranium *rush* was sure the wrong word for his end of the prospecting game. Joe moved back from the edge of the cliff and sat down in the shade of a big pine for a leisurely look around.

Out of the plain directly below and in front of him loomed the Shiprock—a tall mass of dark volcanic stone which had long ago suggested a ship at sea to the pioneers who named it. To Joe it seemed more solitary and surprising than any vessel he had seen on his trips back and forth across the Pacific.

He reckoned that from this spot he could see maybe a hundred miles in three directions. It reminded him of looking out over the plains from the mountains west of Boulder. When he was a kid, he had often felt an intense need of being on high places. Time and again he had climbed mountains to get the big inclusive illusion of seeing everything at once. Now he had the same sensation many times in the copter, and he realized that this was one reason he had taken up flying. A view of a large hunk of the world somehow helped him to sort out his thoughts. Lately they'd needed sorting out, too.

Piloting a whirlybird, he'd thought, would give him a chance to knock around and see more of the world. But what did he expect to find as he drifted about? Joe asked himself the question as he glanced over the empty-looking land below—and he couldn't answer. Maybe if he worked hard and saved his money he could get a copter of his own and go into business. But the thought was vague.

He shifted to a more comfortable position and stretched out full length on the bed of needles under the pine. This was a soft job in some ways, he thought. Better make the most of it until Perry's old man got wise and sent along another Geiger counter for Joe to hike around with. He lazily turned his left wrist so that the face of his watch showed. Eight forty-five. There would be plenty of time later to take care of the bearings.

Joe had nearly dropped off to sleep when the sound of a horse's hoofs made him instantly alert. Coming through the trees behind him was a man on a pinto pony.

Maybe Perry had a good idea when he said the copter shouldn't be left alone with Indians around, Joe thought. But he waved a friendly greeting as he sprang to his feet and pulled out his cigarettes, ready to offer one, crosswise, the way Manny had showed him.

"Howdy," the rider called pleasantly. "Saw this contraption of yours land up here and figured there might be somebody around."

Rats—a white man instead of a Navaho. A little self-consciously Joe put the cigarette between his own lips, loosened another, and pointed the pack at the rider.

"Don't mind if I do," the man said in a soft drawl. "You drive this thing?"

When he had made sure that Joe was the pilot, he became businesslike.

"My name's Worthington," he said. "I came up this morning to check on some horse-branding. That's one of my jobs. I'm district supervisor around here for the Indian Service. I just happened to see what happened at that hogan you almost lit on. Pretty dumb trick—if you don't already know it. You scared a horse there and a kid got throwed."

Worthington stayed in his saddle as he talked. The pleasant note was gone from his voice. "The kid got hurt—hurt bad. One leg is broke, with the bone sticking out."

Joe gave a low whistle of embarrassment and shock. "Did you get a doctor?"

"Get a doctor!" Worthington exploded. "Where do you think you are anyway? That hogan is ten miles from the nearest phone. And there ain't an ambulance nearer than Lukachukai on the other side of the mountain, and it's always out in the field on Thursday—which is today." He paused, then added, "This machine of yours has got to be the ambulance—if you can land it by that hogan."

"I can land all right, but I'm not sure I can take off. It's hot and the air's mighty thin."

"Well, you planned to take off from here, didn't you? Now, if you want to do the right thing, you'll high-tail it for the hospital before that kid gets an infection in his leg. Your fool stunt caused the trouble, and the least you can do is to help the kid out of the mess he's in."

Joe wondered if he ought to explain about the difficulty of flying in the heat of the day, but he decided against it.

"Just so you won't get me into trouble, too," Worthington added, "you might as well know what's what. I don't have any authority to make you take that kid to the hospital. I'm just telling you what's right."

Joe was willing enough to try, but the man's tone got his goat.

"I didn't mean any harm. I just wanted to have a look

at a h-h-hogan," he trailed off uncertainly, realizing that he sounded for all the world like a small boy saying he didn't know the gun was loaded. "I'd never seen one close up."

Worthington let out a snort. "So you pay a call on strangers—just bust in on them from the sky, like a space man from Mars. And then you vamoose and take a siesta!"

There was nothing to say to that. Joe moved awkwardly toward the copter.

"Where's your buddy—the one that does the prospecting?" Worthington asked.

Joe looked up in surprise, partly because he'd forgotten about Perry and partly because this man, who seemed more like a cowboy than a government official, knew about Perry.

"I had word from headquarters in Window Rock that two of you would be up here looking for uranium, and I don't want to leave the other fellow to get lost. Then somebody'd have to hunt for him," the unsmiling horseman explained.

Joe indicated the direction Perry had taken.

"Reckon you can find him and haul him along in this thing?"

"No, he's too far up the hill. And I practically have to stay out of the copter myself to get it off the ground when it's hot this way."

"Well, I'll locate him and show him how to get down to the road. Maybe he can hitch a ride there—or you can come back for him later. There's only one road in this direction. Just follow it if you decide to pick him up."

Then, quickly, Worthington explained how to find the hospital in the town of Shiprock, which lay a dozen miles northeast of the towering mass of lava from which it got its name.

"You put the kid in your machine and light out as quick

as you can. I told his mother to expect you. She don't talk English, by the way, and the kid don't talk it too much. Just be careful how you load him in. The old lady may make quite a fuss and want to come along. Sure you can't take her?"

"Not a chance. Too much weight."

"OK." Worthington turned his horse into the woods. "I don't want to be throwed down off the cliff if my pony happens to take a dislike to that thing-a-ma-jig of yours," he called back with some of the sternness gone from his voice.

CHAPTER 4

The take-off was tricky. Joe opened the throttle wide to get full power out of the engine. He watched the indicator on the tachometer climb up toward the red danger line, and he held the throttle open as the indicator went beyond. At 3400 RPM's he eased up on the stick and let the copter rise a few feet on the cushion of slightly compressed air the rotor had piled up between itself and the rock under the skids. Then he let her settle back down. He wanted to get the exact feel of things before he shot off into empty space.

Again he went up, like a yo-yo on a string. Then, decisively, he maneuvered the sticks and plunged forward and down. An instant after he felt the sagging sensation of the drop, he lowered the pitch of the blades and they sped up. Down he sank as the rotor gathered momentum. Again he gave the blades more pitch—a lot more. With a flash of relief he felt them almost hook into the air.

Once more he lowered the pitch. The blades sped up. And again he checked the fall by changing the pitch. Now he had the control he needed and he skimmed safely out over the tree tops, away from the cliff.

It had been close, and Joe took a deep breath. As the Canary churned off in level flight, he suddenly remembered he hadn't greased the bearings. Well, missing that job one day probably wouldn't do too much damage.

He came down slowly in the clearing around the hogan—

as far from it as he could. And he made sure there was no horse to frighten. What seemed to be a sheep corral was empty. That was good.

The whole place, as a matter of fact, seemed deserted. When he walked over to the hogan, he found the rough door closed.

Joe wondered if the mother had caught the runaway horse and somehow managed to load the boy onto it and start off with him for the hospital. He knocked at the door, though, and waited. He knocked again. Not a sound came from the small six-sided log cabin, and there wasn't a window to look through.

He tried the door, found it unlocked and pushed it open. The mother was there all right, and the two little kids. Lying on a dirty sheepskin at the left, was the boy, his leg in a kind of splint. Blood had stained the strips of cloth that held it in position.

"I came to take your son to the hospital," Joe announced self-consciously. He felt he had to say something, although he remembered very well that the woman couldn't speak English. The two small children crouched behind their mother who sat on the dirt floor. In the dim room all Joe could see of them was the reflection in their eyes of light from the doorway.

No sound came from the mother. The boy was silent, too, but just then he gave an involuntary grunt of pain when he shifted position.

"Mr. Worthington said I should take you to the hospital," Joe spoke directly to the boy now. "I'm sorry I frightened your horse and I'm sorry you got hurt."

The boy didn't answer and Joe looked for some sign of understanding in the strained features of his dark, thin face.

He guessed the youngster might be ten, but small for his age.

Wordlessly he and the Navaho woman eased the sheepskin, with the boy on it, out into the brilliant sunshine. The boy was surprisingly light, but it was a job to hoist him into the cockpit without jarring his leg, which struck out straight in the rude splint. To cushion it, Joe made a bundle of the sheepskin.

After he had strapped the lad into the safety belt, he motioned the mother away. He glanced at her as he set the rotor to spinning, and he thought he had never seen anyone so desolate, yet so far from tears, as this dark woman who stood in her doorway shielding the two younger children behind her ample skirt.

Worthington had apparently done a good job of explaining to her about the helicopter. She had only glanced at the small cockpit and then given up any thought of trying to go along.

The boy was so frightened and in such pain that he kept his eyes closed and his body rigidly motionless as the copter took off. Joe hugged the tops of the scrubby pinyon and juniper growth on the lower slopes. Then for mile after mile he skimmed along above the flat lands, headed toward the San Juan River off to the northeast.

Along its banks a sudden burst of green interrupted the barrens. Giant cottonwoods lined the few short streets that made up the town of Shiprock. Among them Joe easily picked out the bulky white frame hospital, and he found that the parking lot on one side was big enough and empty enough to land in.

As he cut off the engine, Joe glanced at the tense boy beside him. Only now did the youngster open his eyes.

"Be right back," Joe said, touching his arm lightly. "You'll feel better in a little while."

He swung down out of the cockpit and looked about him. The brown faces of little girls stared at him from windows all along the near side of the building. Behind them was a brown-skinned woman in a blue uniform.

Inside, a few Navahos stood in front of an Indian woman who seemed to be kind of receptionist. Joe's confused impulse was to join the line and not rush ahead of these people, who looked as if they'd been waiting a long time. No, that didn't make sense.

"I've got a boy outside with a compound fracture," he said to the attendant with urgency in his voice.

"I'll find someone," the woman replied and was off down the corridor at what Joe thought a criminally slow pace. But in a moment a young white girl appeared. Her starched uniform rustled as she walked rapidly toward him.

"Where's the patient?" she asked, then in almost the same breath she instructed the Navaho woman to find the head nurse. For the first time since Worthington broke into his siesta, Joe relaxed.

After two stout young Navaho men lifted the injured boy onto a stretcher and carried him off through a pair of swinging doors, Joe slumped down on a bench in the corridor.

"Please wait here," the young nurse said.

The receptionist took care of the waiting Navahos, and one by one they either left or went farther into the hospital. Soon the receptionist herself disappeared and Joe was alone.

Somewhere a typewriter rattled, and occasionally he heard a woman's voice taking calls on the telephone. The only other sound he could distinguish above the suppressed murmur of the place was a booming baritone voice. It came from beyond the swinging doors where the patients all seemed to be, and the words weren't English. Probably Navaho.

Another male voice seemed to be engaged in conversation with the baritone. When both broke out in hearty laughter, Joe wished he could be in on the joke. He was plenty bored just sitting.

A few more unintelligible sounds came from behind the swinging doors, and a big, heavy-set, middle-aged white man in a light summer suit pushed them apart. He nodded pleasantly at Joe, then stopped.

"You being taken care of?" he asked, seeming to note that there was no receptionist.

"Thanks, I'm OK," Joe replied. "I'm just waiting to hear about an Indian kid I brought in."

"Who is it?"

Joe wondered at the stranger's interest. "Some kid with a broken leg. Don't know his name. I just brought him in."

The man looked keenly at Joe. "You new around here? My name's Reed."

Joe introduced himself. The man's handshake was as hearty as his voice. In a moment Joe found himself telling what had happened. Reed stepped to the doorway and looked out at the Canary.

"We could use some of those things on the reservation right now," he said enthusiastically. "Transportation is one of our biggest headaches. There aren't half enough roads, and half the time the ones we have are impassable. Congress would be smart to give us money for a batch of those machines."

With that the man grinned and called, "So long." Out in

the parking lot, after a curious look at the Canary, he stepped into a car labelled "United States Indian Service" and drove off.

Joe sat down again with his elbows on his knees and his head in his hands. No telling how long he'd have to wait. . . .

"Would you please step into the office?" The words came rapidly. Joe hadn't realized anyone was standing in front of him. He looked up at the young nurse he had seen before. His first impression had been only of starched efficiency. Now he saw a pleasant round face smiling at him from under a ridiculous nurse's cap. But the starched efficiency was still there. She wasted no time in beginning to ask questions.

The boy's name? Joe didn't know.

Where did he live? Joe couldn't describe the exact location, but he could point it out on a map.

How did the accident happen? That was easy—but not really easy at all. Joe had to admit he buzzed the hogan—a thing he knew he should not do to any house anywhere. He might lose his pilot's license for an irresponsible stunt like that. Worthington had made him feel that there was something especially wrong about buzzing a hogan. The district supervisor's brief, acid words of criticism still rankled, and part of Joe fought back against them. What made Navahos different from anybody else? Are they so dumb that the sight of a good modern machine like a helicopter scares them to death? If they are that dumb, why worry about how they feel? . . . But another part of him knew that a copter or plane can scare a lot of people. He'd seen it happen many times while he did his brief stretch in Korea. He hadn't been a pilot there, just a mechanic working on trucks and jeeps. But he'd seen Koreans run like frightened turkeys when a copter hovered overhead or landed near them. . . . And when you came right down to it, the kid's horse was really the one that had been most frightened. Anybody can get bucked off a scared horse. He'd been thrown more than once when he was a kid.

In spite of his tangled thoughts and emotions, Joe told his story of the accident and managed to get in the admission that he was to blame.

"Joseph Fraser, 21, transient. Mail address: R.D., Cortez, Colorado. Employed as helicopter pilot by the Colorado and Western Mining Co. . . ." The nurse put all the facts down, then explained, "The head nurse said to get this for the records. Incidentally, the Navaho Police may want to talk to you." Then she added a little bitterly, "I don't think you need to worry, though, since you're working for that uranium company. They'll fix it so you won't be in any trouble, and nobody will have to pay any damages. Only the government will have to pay the hospital bill, and we haven't got beds enough as it is."

"Are you always as sarcastic and sour as that?" Joe asked bristling. "Or only when a guy comes and admits he made a mistake?"

The nurse rose, blushing, from behind the bare desk on which she had been taking her notes. As she started to speak, Joe realized for the first time that she was not very tall—a good eight inches shorter than he.

"I'm sorry," she said. "I didn't mean it the way it sounded. I've only been here a few months—since I finished nursing school—and I guess I haven't learned how to take it yet. I have to go back on the floor now," she added, trying to regain her composure. "Seems like I have to be everywhere at once. So long."

"Any law that says I can't hang around to hear what the sawbones says about the kid?" Joe called after her as she strode energetically down the corridor.

"Wait here," she replied with a cheerful note in her voice that surprised Joe. "I'll give you the dope. By the way I'm Miss Ericson—Beth Ericson." And she disappeared through the swinging doors. Joe was left there surrounded only by the pervasive antiseptic hospital odor he had hated ever since he'd had pneumonia in the army.

CHAPTER 5

Perry stretched his arms out over sheets of paper on the collapsible aluminum table, protecting them from the Canary's downwash, when Joe landed in the open space among the pinyons where they had set up their field camp. As soon as the papers ceased to rustle, Perry continued work on them. An awning extended from their trailer and shielded his eyes from the last direct rays of the late afternoon sun, which slid down along the eastern slope of the Chuskas.

"That government cowboy tell you why I had to go awol on you?" Joe called from under the dying swish of the rotor. He figured Perry might be sore because he ran off with the copter and left him stranded.

But Perry, absorbed in his work, just grunted.

"Get a hitch down all right?"

"A truck brought me down almost as soon as I reached the road," Perry said matter-of-factly. Then a trace of excitement livened up his flat voice as he went on. "Lucky thing I had to hike. Look what I found." He pointed to a chunk of pale yellow rock on the table.

"Carnotite!" Joe burst out. He had seen samples of the uranium-bearing ore for which Perry was hunting.

"It's carnotite all right, and the Geiger counter shows

it's pretty high grade for this area," Perry said with more reserve than enthusiasm.

Why can't that guy work up some real excitement? Joe wondered. In his place I'd be shouting so seven counties could hear me.

"Where'd you find it?" Joe held the gritty specimen out in the sunlight where its yellow seemed more intense.

Perry hesitated as he tried to think of recognizable landmarks. "About four hundred yards south and down the mountain from the cliff we landed on this morning," he answered. "Here—I made a grid survey."

Perry held out a sheet of paper on which lines cut at crazy angles between other lines laid out in perfect squares. Joe knew that Perry, in his methodical way, had paced off the whole area around his strike, taking Geiger counter readings at regular intervals. The lines on the squared paper showed what the counter had revealed. They indicated the rough contour of the ore deposit he had found.

"How big do you figure the deposit is?" Joe asked as he tried to interpret the lines.

"Big, I think," was Perry's reply, "but there's no telling really. See how the readings shade down all around here." His pencil touched on an irregular area centering around the location of the outcrop. "My counter won't pick up radiations when the ore is under more than two feet of overburden. The deposit may stop here, or it may extend a long distance in any direction under the sandstone."

At last things were going to happen the way Joe had expected them to in a mining boom. Test-drill rigs, bulldozers, miners—they'd bring some life and action to this lonely mountainside. He could already see the trucks streaming down a new road, full of the yellow ore, a million dollars worth of it—ten million—why not?

"The first strike!" he groaned. "And I had to miss it." Then a sudden thought filled him with alarm. "Sure nobody's already staked out a claim there?"

"I found a cairn and some stakes not far away, but they didn't include my strike."

Joe knew that a cairn was a pile of stones which a prospector always built at the point where he discovered valuable mineral. All at once he had vision of himself piling up a cairn, setting out stakes to mark the boundaries of a claim of his own, filling out a claim form and nailing it to a post—so that anyone who came by would know that Joe Fraser had made his strike.

"I put up my stakes and made out my claim papers," Perry said. "I only had time to pace off a couple of acres, but that'll do for now. Dad will probably want to send in a drilling rig to test the whole area before we file for the nine hundred sixty acres we're entitled to."

"What did you name her?" Joe broke in. A prospector always gave a name to his claim and put it on his form.

"The Hike-Down, because I was walking down the mountain. It was all I could think of at the time."

Joe was amused, then dismayed. The mine would probably be called the Hike-Down, too—a lasting reminder that he and the Canary had not been around as they should have been when Perry made his strike.

"Tomorrow I'm filing at Window Rock," Perry went on. "Then I'm going to the ranch. I want to assay this stuff and get in touch with Dad. He'll want to have men in here right away."

"And then I'll have a day off. Tomorrow makes nine straight days of flying."

"We'll see."

"What do you mean, we'll see?" Joe still wasn't used to having Perry decide things for him. And in his books, if you worked you deserved time off, no matter who you worked for.

But Perry had no interest in an argument. He was lost again in his maps and figures.

If I yelled "Fire!" right now, I bet he'd just say, "Well, put it out." I'd be painting the town red if I'd made a strike like this. Pure luck, too. He just stumbled on it. I could do it myself, if—yes, if.

All of a sudden Joe knew that Mr. Burns had been very shrewd. Uranium fever could sure get you. Any strike Joe made belonged to the company, period. A lot of good that would do him. Of course, he could quit his job and go off prospecting somewhere else. But he'd be a heel to run out on Perry right now. He'd told Perry he'd help him for the summer.

Joe kicked at the ground in disgust, went over to the jeep, and turned on the radio—loud. The Gallup station was just closing its late afternoon Navaho hour, and the eerie falsetto of an Indian chant filled the clearing. The weird, monotonous music was no oil for Joe's troubled waters. It reminded him of the Navaho kid's broken leg. The nurse at the hospital had said they'd have to keep the youngster for a while to make sure no complications set in.

Perry hadn't even asked about the kid or about the trip to the hospital. The Lucky Break—that ought to be the name for his claim. Oh, well— Joe turned the radio dial until he found a dance band. He snapped his fingers and shuffled his feet restlessly on the adobe soil in time to the music. . . .

It was Joe's turn to cook supper on the gasoline stove in the trailer's little galley, and Perry's turn to wash dishes. While Perry was finishing his part of the chore, Joe had an idea that struck him as brilliant.

"Hey, Perry, doesn't the first strike of your career call for a big blowout? How about taking Pat and Helen-May out dancing when we get back to the ranch?"

Perry looked startled. Celebration wasn't much in his line. But this one would be hard to get out of. On an occasion like this his father would certainly want him to do a little public relations work with Arnold Spencer's daughter. Joe saw with glee that Perry had stepped into his trap.

"Not a bad idea," Perry said, a little glumly. "You line up the girls."

Next morning early they started out for Window Rock, where the Navaho tribe and the Indian Service had their headquarters. Soon after the take-off, Joe saw the hogan he'd buzzed the day before. Only a dim, winding wagon track led up to the place. If the kid went home from the hospital in a wagon, the trip would take the better part of a day. The Canary could get him there in twenty minutes. It might be a nice idea to give him a lift—if Joe could wangle it somehow with Perry.

"The kid will have to stay in the hospital a while—they're scared of infection," he shouted to Perry at his side.

"What kid?" Perry looked blank.

"The boy that got his leg broken yesterday when I buzzed that hogan."

"Oh, yes," was all Perry said.

In real perplexity, Joe took his eyes off the country ahead and turned to study his companion. What was happening to this guy? There was no easy answer to the question. Perry had been right there when the kid got hurt, and he wasn't even interested. Joe looked out again for the landmarks he had to follow. He didn't know the country, but there was no way of getting lost. As long as he had the black-topped Highway 666 on his left and the green woods and red-orange mountains of sandstone on his right, he was OK.

A couple of dirt roads and occasional wagon tracks passed under him, and three or four times he saw tiny clusters of buildings. None of them were big enough to be villages on most maps, but settlements out here were so few and far between that his aviation chart listed them all—Anostee, Tacito, Two Gray Hills, Tohatchi. Otherwise there was nothing but the reddish earth dotted with little tufts of stubborn vegetation and slashed deeply from time to time by gullies. People around here called them washes—a mild term for what violent erosion did to the landscape.

"Copter sure is the only way to travel," Joe shouted and pointed down at one particularly nasty wash that seemed to threaten the highway like an open, spreading wound. One good cloudburst could chew right through the blacktop and cut off all traffic between Shiprock and Gallup. Then, with a look at the looming Chuskas on his right, he added confidently, "Won't be long before they put superchargers on. Then we can hop over mountains higher than those." The Canary in flight was no place for conversation, but Joe felt like talking and he kept on. "How does anybody make a living around here?" He pointed with his head toward a hogan surrounded by land too barren to keep a jackrabbit alive.

Perry shrugged. "Mostly sheep," he yelled. "That's all they know, but they overgraze. Ruin the land."

Ahead Joe could see Highway 68 threading its way west through a pass in the low ridge of red sandstone, to which the Chuskas had now dwindled. He followed it, and before long he located a neat collection of low masonry buildings, sheltered on three sides by sandstone cliffs. One of the rock formations had a great round hole through it—the Window Rock. From here the hole looked big enough to fly through, and Joe had a crazy notion to try it. But he set the Canary down not far from the main Indian Service building and waited while Perry went into file his papers. Funny guy—he'd taken his time about getting into the field, but now he probably held some kind of speed record for filing a claim. It was only eight fifteen, the morning after he'd made his strike, and here he was with papers already at headquarters, thanks to Joe and the Canary.

Office workers, Navaho and white, gathered at the windows of the one-story headquarters building and stared at the copter. A few Navaho men began to drift cautiously out of the nearest doorway. Before the diffident sightseers had reached the Canary, an Indian Service car drove up and a big man stepped from it.

"Hello, Mr. Reed," Joe called.

"You sure do get around in that egg-beater," Reed replied with cheerful admiration.

"You seem to get around yourself."

"Part of my job," Reed said. "Civil service has got me in the wrong classification. They'd save a lot of money if they paid me to be a chauffeur instead of a stuffed shirt. I spend half my time behind the wheel—or with a shovel in my hand digging out of some mud hole."

Reed seemed to know everybody in the small crowd which was oozing toward the copter. He greeted each one by name, speaking sometimes in Navaho and sometimes in English.

With a little feeling of regret, Joe sensed that Reed was soaking up questions that would have been his to answer if Reed hadn't appeared. It would be interesting to talk to the Navahos. Only one of them wore his hair long the way Manny did, and the crown of his hat rose up in a dome. The others had all flattened or creased theirs across the top. One man stood a full six feet two in his cowboy boots. Another, in a loud sport shirt, was short and dumpy. Several were slender and of medium height. And they ranged in complexion from tan to mahogany.

It was too soon for any of the Indians to break away from Reed and come over to the Canary when Perry strode out of the building, head forward and legs lagging behind as usual. He was ready to go.

"Everything OK with the claim?" Joe inquired.

"It's ours all right, but Dad'll be sore."

This didn't make sense, and Joe said so.

"There's that other claim I told you about right close to ours. The office says it shows high-grade ore. Dad'll want it, too."

"Oh, he can lease it or buy it or something." Perry could worry about the strangest things.

A group of Navahos was headed for an odd-shaped masonry structure nearby that Joe hadn't noticed before. Heavy beam-ends jutted out through its many-sided walls at intervals below a second story set back from the first.

"Looks something like an overgrown hogan," Joe said as Perry fastened his safety belt.

"I think that's where the Tribal Council meets," Perry said.

"The what?"

"Council. It hasn't much real power, but it can make trouble for the uranium industry all the same."

"How come?"

"It tries to get favored treatment for Navaho prospectors. An Indian staked out the claim next to mine."

Joe started the engine and headed back along the route by which he had come. With the extra gas he carried, he could easily make the hundred and seventy miles to the Spencer ranch by noon.

Chapter 6

Joe worked up a good lather in his thick brown hair and then stood under the shower. As he twisted and turned under the hot spray he marveled at the murky water flowing past his feet into the drain. This desert dust was really insidious stuff.

He switched off the hot, turned the cold on full force, and snorted from the shock of it. Nothing like a good cold shower. This ranch really did things right. Cold water and a lot of pressure in a private bathroom.

At home, one old-fashioned tub served the whole household and there was no pressure to speak of. Just gravity flow from a tank in the attic. Warm water always came out of the cold faucet in the summer. . . . Old man Spencer must have had all the breaks.

Joe hurried into a T shirt and a clean pair of jeans. Below his window the cook beat the iron triangle which hung outside the kitchen door. That meant there would be no chance to corner the girls before the noon dinner.

There was of course no chance to speak during dinner either. After the usual dessert of apple pie, Joe headed for the screened-in porch. That would be the place to talk to the girls. Perry and Spencer and Buss Gillmore, who was still around—or else back again—settled down in the living-room and Joe could hear Perry telling about his strike.

Suddenly Joe had an idea. Perry's Geiger counter and the carnotite specimen lay on the porch table. Backing up to the table, Joe pushed the carnotite under the Denver *Post* spread out over it. Then he looked as earnest and enthusiastic as he could.

"Say, do you gals want to try a scientific experiment? Perry and I tried it this week and we found out something that may be important."

Pat was up on her toes with interest. "What do we do?" she asked.

"Let me explain something first," Joe said with professorial solemnity. "Perry and I were sitting around the campfire one night and this Geiger counter started to click. It was right beside me. Perry experimented, and he discovered I was radioactive. He says some people are. The machine wouldn't click for him at all. He's normal. Do you want me to find out if either of you is radioactive?"

"Is it dangerous to be?" Pat wanted to know.

"That depends," Joe said, playing it straight. "You walk slowly toward me and we'll find out whether you're normal or abnormal."

Pat began to take little steps toward Joe. He switched on the Geiger counter and adjusted the earphones. As Pat moved closer and closer, she began to tease him for his report.

"Put these on and listen." Joe handed over the earphones when Pat had reached the table where the carnotite specimen lay.

"I click like crazy," Pat squealed with excitement.

"You sure do," was Joe's solemn pronouncement. "Now let's see. . . ."

He took the counter over to Helen-May, who hadn't

budged from her comfortable couch. Waving the probe in the air over and around her, Joe listened, then he handed the earphones to Pat.

"Not a sound," Pat announced with some caution. She listened again. Then, "Oh Helen, you're normal!" she said triumphantly. "But what about me? Is it dangerous the way I am?"

"For short periods, there's no danger," Joe answered. "But it wouldn't be safe if you stayed close to a non-radioactive person very long."

He knew he had carried things far enough—perhaps too far. He'd better clinch the date for tonight.

"For instance," he said. "Perry made a big uranium strike yesterday—"

"Oh, how exciting—" Pat began.

"Hold everything," Joe interrupted. "Tonight he's celebrating—at a dance or something in Durango. Naturally he wants you two in on the fun. But it might be bad for Helen-May if she sat next to me in the car all the way to Durango and back. Or bad for Perry if Pat sat next to him. It's perfectly safe for us to trade dances, of course."

To Joe's surprise Helen-May exploded. Probably he wasn't the first guy who'd tried to side-track her.

"You're nothing but a cad!" she said, exactly the way a virtuous maiden would talk in an old-fashioned melodrama, and she spoke her line with such unlikely vigor that Joe couldn't laugh. "I saw you hide something under that newspaper." Helen-May was angry all up and down her nearly six-foot long body.

"You just tried a trick so you could take Pat, who's the right height for Perry, not you. Serves you right anyway." Her high voice carried conviction. "We can't *either* of us go with you. Mr. Spencer is flying us in to Gallup this afternoon to catch the plane for Dallas. Then we're going to Europe with my folks."

Helen-May got up and strode majestically into the house.

Pat slipped into the living-room after her, but in a minute she was back.

"Perry says there's no such thing," she announced, not looking at all angry.

"No such thing as what?" Joe asked innocently.

"You know. Radioactive people." Pat hesitated. "Anyway it was a nice idea—and not nice," she added, flashing her eyes upward toward the second story where Helen-May was presumably sulking in her room. "Maybe if you're still here when we get back from Europe . . ." Pat's words trailed off. She scampered into the house again.

Joe sagged down in a chair to survey the ruins of his scheme for a big evening. At least Pat's response to his dopey trick had been flattering. But there was a long summer ahead and she wouldn't be around.

He had to admit, he'd been rough on Helen-May, but how was he to know she was bright enough to see him hide the carnotite? Maybe he should think twice before trying some of his spur-of-the-moment stunts. But what are you supposed to do about a dopey dame like that?

For a while he just sat and looked out over the rich green stretch of lawn in front of the house. Beyond was an alfalfa field almost ready for its first mowing.

"These Indians don't know how to use what they've got and they never will," Spencer was saying in the living-room. Joe could hear his words clearly through the open window. "We've got to do the job, but this system of pampering them is holding us back. If the Bureau of Indian Affairs would just fold up and give each Indian his own piece of land, things would be different. In no time at all, whites with capital and modern methods would be developing the area. And, believe me, there's potential wealth there."

"Arnold, you're too impatient," Gillmore said. "The government is solving the problem. We are freeing the Indian, as we say."

Joe wondered what "freeing" the Indian could mean. Perry asked the question for him: "I thought they all got citizenship a few years back. Didn't they?"

"Yes, yes," Gillmore answered. "I mean we have to give them the right to sell their land if they want to. That means getting rid of the reservations and tribal councils and the Indian Service, too. We've made some progress. We've already got special protection removed from several tribes. It's only a question of time before we'll free the Navahos, too."

"I'm not as optimistic as you are," Spencer said. "There's been a lot of sentimental publicity about the 'plight of the Navahos.' "

"There'll be some hullaballoo, no doubt. But don't worry. We'll handle that when the time comes."

Gillmore lapsed into silence.

Joe heard Perry making a phone call in the office that adjoined the living-room.

"Dad'll be here Monday night with a crew," Perry announced when he came back to join the older men.

That reminded Joe: He'd better grease the bearings on the copter.

CHAPTER 7

As Joe left the house, on his way to the Canary, he discovered Manny having the time of his life following a gasoline mower around the lawn.

"Hi, Manny!" he called. The young Navaho didn't hear above the loud explosions of the one-cylinder engine. He kept on walking behind the self-propelled machine—his fluid gait in curious contrast to the regularity of the put-puts that came from the exhaust.

"Hey! Manny!" Joe shouted louder. This time Manny heard and killed the engine. Smiling, he came over and offered a limp hand. Joe still wasn't used to the boneless grip. Did all Navahos shake hands this way? Sometime he'd find a way to ask about it. . . . Manny wasn't exactly a husky, and he was a good deal shorter than Joe, but he was every inch bone and lean, lithe muscle—nothing like his handclasp.

"Mr. Spencer said his mower was no good. Wouldn't work." Manny's shyness didn't conceal a sense of triumph. Joe couldn't tell whether the victory was over the machine, or over Spencer, or both.

"How about lending me a hand on the copter?" Joe asked. "I've got to grease the bearings."

Manny was willing, and the two of them worked together as smoothly as a well-trained team.

"What do you want to wrangle horses for?" Joe said when

they had finished. "You're a good mechanic. Why don't you get a job in a garage or someplace?"

"I tried."

Something in Manny's voice told Joe he had entered unpleasant territory, so he switched the subject. Soon he found himself talking about the boy with the broken leg and his own dumb stunt of buzzing a hogan. Could Manny find out who the kid was—and what Joe could do to make amends?

"I'll see," was the vague answer.

Joe pressed the point. He took out an aviation chart and indicated where the hogan was. Still Manny had nothing to say, although Joe was sure he could read a map, from the intense way he studied it.

The grease job didn't take long but it was hot work, for there was no shade over the Canary. Joe went to the kitchen and got two coke bottles out of one of the big refrigerators.

"This goes good," Manny finally said, as he drained the last of the chilly liquid from the bottle Joe had given him.

"Hear about Perry's luck?" Joe asked in an effort to keep the conversation going.

"What's that?"

"He made a big uranium strike up on the mountain—not far from the place where that kid I told you about lives. Filed his claim this morning in Window Rock."

"I got a claim up there too," Manny announced—with a tight quality in his voice.

"No kidding! Why aren't you working it?"

"I'm waiting for my prize. An assayer in Gallup told me I had the best uranium ore he'd seen. Washington offered a ten-thousand-dollar prize to anybody who made a big uranium discovery."

"Ten grand—that ain't hay!"

Manny wiped the grease off his hands and dug his wallet out of the hip pocket of his levis. From it he took a badly frayed newspaper clipping. About all Joe could make out was the headline: AEC OFFERS $10,000 FOR BIG URANIUM FIND.

"I'm still waiting to get it," Manny said. "They say I wrote to the wrong place every other time. When the money comes, I can start a real mine."

The uranium fever flared up in Joe again. Ten thousand bucks, right off the bat, just waiting to be found. Even Manny could make a strike.

"How'd you do it? Geiger counter?" Joe asked.

"No. The same way many Navahos did. I was in a trading post after I got out of the service—over at Lukachukai. A man from Washington came by and showed us some specimens. He said we would get money if we told him where more rocks like that could be found. I remembered where I'd seen some. A long time ago I was helping some brothers—I guess you'd call them cousins. They had sheep on the mountains up above there. So I went back to the place."

"Well, what d'ya know!"

"But I didn't tell the government man. Some of the others did, and they weren't paid much money. I found out how to file a claim, and I read in the paper about the ten-thousand-dollar prize for a big new strike. Mine was big," Manny said with assurance.

Joe knew that in the Colorado mining districts you had to make improvements on a claim in order to keep it. He asked how it was on the Reservation.

"I claimed about four acres. So I have to do twenty dollars' worth of work this year. I still have a little time before my year runs out."

"That's good," Joe said the words, but only part of his mind was on them. A fine box he'd put himself in. Here he was, in the middle of a country full of uranium, and he couldn't go looking for it on his own. . . .

Mr. Spencer called Manny to carry the traveling bags to the Navion. The girls were all dressed up now, and Pat looked right out of Hollywood. She wanted to give Joe a good-by handshake, but he wouldn't let her. He was too greasy.

Buss Gillmore had decided to go along for the ride. At the last minute Perry came out dutifully to see the party leave. He's the lucky one, Joe thought. He gets out of a celebration he didn't want anyway.

After the Navion took off, Perry disappeared and Manny drove away in the ranch truck to pick up the mail which would soon arrive. Joe's thoughts turned to the long empty evening ahead. He might phone and ask that nurse Beth Ericson about the boy in the hospital. That was his only idea, and he acted on it, making a note of the cost of the call. He'd pay Spencer for it later.

About all the nurse said in her cool, low voice was that the kid seemed fine, and she hoped Joe would come to visit him. This wasn't very big news, but it gave Joe an excuse for talking to Manny. Perry was busy doing tests and wouldn't want to be bothered. After supper Joe went out to Manny's cabin. It was a one-room affair, separate from the large bunkhouse where the regular cowhands slept and ate when they were on the place. Manny didn't answer when he knocked.

Joe wandered to the kitchen, and the cook told him Manny hadn't been in for supper. He'd brought back the mail and left it on Spencer's desk. After that she hadn't seen him. It was the first time he'd ever missed a meal.

Joe looked around behind the implement shed where Manny kept his own pick-up truck. It wasn't there. He returned to the cabin, and this time he opened the door. Obviously Manny had cleared out.

Joe sat down on the rough board bunk. What cooked with that guy anyway? Maybe Spencer said something that made him sore. Of course, he'd gone for the mail. He could have got a letter calling him home. Uncommunicative though Manny was, Joe had formed a clear picture of a mother and several brothers and sisters to whom he was deeply attached. . . .

Joe was irritated—nobody to talk to on the whole place. As he started to leave the cabin, he noticed a crumpled bit of paper on the floor. Without much curiosity he picked it up. It was a letter to Manuelito Begay—that must be Manny—on Atomic Energy Commission stationery. The guy who signed it had a title a mile long, but he only said that Manny had been mistaken about the ten-thousand-dollar award. There was an award or bonus all right, but it did not apply to finds in the Colorado Plateau, which included the Chuska Mountains where Manny had his claim.

Manny was sore and had gone off in a huff. Joe was sure of that. He would have been plenty sore himself.

CHAPTER 8

Just after dawn the next day, Joe shuttled Perry back to the field camp, and then up to the cliff above the claim. There he was amused to see Perry face a difficult decision: Whether to leave Joe as usual baby-sitting with the copter, or to leave it unattended and bring Joe along to help him do some leg work.

Perry had made up his mind to claim all the area into which the deposit he had found might possibly extend. Obviously he wanted to impress his father—and his father's experts—with a good job, and it would help a lot if Joe came along to pile up cairns with stakes in them wherever he decided they should go. On the other hand Perry knew his father would be furious if anything happened to the Canary.

Joe came to his rescue. "Leave the copter today. Nothing's going to happen to it. Navahos have been scarce as hens' teeth along these cliffs all the time we've been flying up here. And I don't think they'd bother the machine anyway. Why in the world should they?" As Joe spoke he realized that he looked forward to a little active exercise. He was glad when Perry, still looking worried, decided to take his advice.

They spent the day scrambling up and down steep slopes, piling stones around weathered pine branches which were to serve as stakes. Perry was entitled to claim nine hundred and sixty acres and seemed driven to cover as much of that very large hunk of mountainside as he could in one day. Joe was getting a work-out for sure.

At one point Perry showed him the cairn marking the outcropping of ore on the Indian claim he had discovered near his own. Joe lifted a flat stone and found a tin can. In it was the claim form. When he saw the name of the prospector he let out a low whistle. Manuelito Begay—Manny! There couldn't be two Manuelito Begays who had uranium claims in the Chuskas. He glanced at the date on the form. Manny had less than three weeks before the year would be up. He had to make his improvements right away—start sinking a shaft, or whack out a piece of road—if he wanted to keep his claim. Maybe that was why he quit his job. He might be coming up here any day to start work.

It was a good claim all right. Perry had checked and double-checked it with his Geiger counter. Perhaps there was a big body of ore in the mountain connecting his own strike with this Indian's. Anyway Perry extended a row of stakes tentatively all around Manny's—and far beyond.

It's none of my business, Joe thought, but life might be real interesting around here if Manny turns up. Not that Perry was claim-jumping. He had just outlined territory that surrounded Manny's four acres. But Joe had a hunch that Manny, in his own way, would be a match for Perry if it came to an argument.

Apparently in studying Manny's claim form, Perry had missed the fact that he actually knew the prospector who had left it there. Joe himself had learned Manny's full name only by chance—and he certainly wasn't going to volunteer the information. It occurred to him, though, to find out something about the government-award business.

"Wouldn't a good strike like yours—or this other one up

here—be good for the ten-thousand-dollar prize the AEC offers for a major new strike?" he asked Perry.

"Oh, that," Perry said. "Not a chance. That offer got spread all over the papers, and hundreds—maybe thousands—of prospectors started out into the field with Geiger counters. Some of them made good strikes, too, but nobody in this area got the ten thousand dollars—or ever will."

"Sounds as if there's some dirty business somewhere," was Joe's blunt observation.

"The trouble was most prospectors didn't read the actual

announcement of the bonus—that's what it was called. They just read the newspapers, which made it sound sensational. The bonus offer specifically excluded the whole Colorado Plateau—where the AEC already knew there was uranium. It wasn't a new field."

"I still think it was a dirty trick. The AEC should have made the papers straighten out the stories."

"It's hardly the AEC's fault if people don't take the trouble to find out facts. Besides, they got a lot of prospecting done, and that's what counts."

Joe wasn't impressed, but he had discovered something he'd like to tell Manny. He dimly suspected Manny thought the award had been denied him solely because he was an Indian. If Joe only had some idea where Manny might be, he'd run over to see him some evening and drop this bit of news. Also, he'd remind the guy to shake a leg and do his improvement work, if he wasn't already planning to. . . .

That night before supper Joe borrowed the jeep and went down toward the highway, then off on a rutty road he didn't know. The nearest trading post—hence the nearest phone—lay that way.

The good-natured Irish trader, Peter Brannan, was just closing up, but he let Joe in to use the phone. Joe studied the bewildering variety of stuff in the store as he waited for the operator to get the hospital at Shiprock: Manufactured blankets—"Pendleton" blankets—in garish colors and conventional designs. Lariats, cowboy boots, some of them very small—obviously for kids. Cases full of candy bars. Crates and crates of empty pop bottles. A pile of sheepskins. Flashlights, autochains, yard goods, shelves of groceries—mostly in cans. A large, very modern-looking refrigerated showcase holding a few chunks of mutton.

The call finally went through, and he had Beth Ericson on the wire.

Yes, the boy's leg was doing very well. They probably would release him in three or four days. There had been a lot of trouble finding out his name. At first he wouldn't tell it to anybody—even to the Navaho interpreters. But a young "long hair"—that's what she called a Navaho who wore his hair in a bun—had come to see the boy. After the visit he had told the hospital that the youngster's name was Billie Begay.

When had the "long-hair" been in? Last night at visiting time. What were the visiting hours? Between seven and eight in the evening and three to four in the afternoon. . . .

The "long-hair" must be Manny. He'd had time enough to get from the ranch to the hospital by seven. Manuelito Begay —Billie Begay: there must be a connection.

Joe told the nurse he wanted to come and see Billie tomorrow afternoon. He could probably get at least part of the day off. After all it would be Sunday, and Memorial Day.

As he hung up he had a vague feeling of dissatisfaction with the call. He realized he had wanted to do more than just find out about the kid. He'd wanted some conversation with Beth Ericson—and she'd been too businesslike. Maybe she could act a little more human when she was off duty. Tomorrow he'd have another chance to talk to her and find out what her hours were. It might be worth while trying for a date.

"Do you happen to know a kid by the name of Billie Begay?" Joe thought to ask the trader as he moved toward the heavy door.

"Sure, I know the family. They always graze their sheep on this side of the mountain in summertime. Got some of his mother's pawn right here."

Brannan pointed to a rafter from which hung a long line of silver concha belts, turquoise necklaces, and silver and turquoise bracelets. He fingered the cardboard identification tags that dangled from the jewelry.

Brannan stopped at one belt made of beautifully designed conchas, each one the circumference of a big orange, and said, "This belt belongs to the kid's mother. She's having a tough time now that he's gone—I heard about his leg. He did most of the herding of her sheep and goats. Her husband died early this spring of TB."

"Does this Billie have an older brother or a relative named Manuelito?" Joe asked.

"No brother. I'm sure of that. I wouldn't know all his other relatives. You never do with Navahos," Brannan said.

"I know a Manuelito Begay who has been around here. Thought he and the kid might be related since they both have the same name."

The trader smiled. "That Begay business fools a lot of people. It just means 'son of.' It's not a family name like Smith or Brannan. Your Manuelito may be the son of a man called Manuelito. On the other hand, some dumb schoolteacher may have heard that Manuelito's father was called something-or-other Begay, and so she tacked the name onto all the man's kids. I happen to know that's why Billie's whole family is called Begay."

"Whoa, there," Joe interrupted. "You mean Navahos only have one name?"

"As a matter of fact, they often have two or three different ones—and a white man almost never knows a Navaho's *real* name. He keeps that to himself and doesn't use it. Using it wears it out and makes it lose its magical power. But they only have last names because teachers or traders or other white people insist. We all think the world will come to an end unless everybody does just the way we do. . . ."

Joe was thoughtful as he headed back toward camp.

"You're late," Perry said accusingly when Joe entered the trailer, "and it's your turn to cook supper."

"Keep your shirt on, Perry. I'm sorry—the trip took longer than I figured." Joe hurried the supper as fast as he could. It was all out of tin cans.

As the two ate in the tiny compartment which served as their living-room, bedroom, and dining-room, Joe said, "I'm going to the hospital tomorrow to see that Indian kid. Can I have the jeep?"

"You had the jeep today and you were late getting back," Perry said flatly.

"I told you I was sorry, but I had to get to the trading post before it closed." Joe wished he hadn't apologized. He had a right to some time off.

"And I could use you all day tomorrow," Perry went on as if he hadn't heard. "I want to find out everything I can about the area around my strike before Dad gets here."

"Look, Perry, we've worked every day for nearly two weeks. Do I get time off, or do you expect me to be on the job every day all summer long? If you do, you've another guess coming."

"When we offered you the job, Dad and I thought you'd take a real interest in it," Perry said stiffly, looking a good more like his father than Joe had ever seen him look before.

Joe studied Perry with real perplexity. When they had camped out as kids, there had never been a conversation like this.

"I guess we should have talked about it before this trip

started," Joe said, wanting to avoid a head-on collision. "But we didn't. So let's straighten it out now. I'll work in a pinch whenever you need me, you know that. But I can't see why you're in an uproar about tomorrow. There's no sense in spending any more time on that claim. Your dad's crew will go over everything again anyway. So how about it?"

"Something might turn up so that I'd want the jeep."

"Something like what?" Joe was having trouble keeping his temper. "I'd be glad to take the copter, if you'd rather. I just thought it was more sensible to leave that here and drive down to Shiprock. You know, Perry, it would do you good to knock off tomorrow and lie around camp or go to town with me."

"You don't seem to understand. There's a job to do here."

"You didn't figure I'd be on tap every minute of the day or night, did you? Besides, I signed up as a pilot—not as a prospector."

"Well, I guess it'll be all right this time," Perry said. "I suppose I can use the time to work up my field notes."

The next day Joe drove into the hospital yard promptly at three. After seeing the kid, he would try to see Beth Ericson.

The Navaho receptionist recognized Joe, but she couldn't tell him where to find Miss Ericson. She was off duty and definitely wasn't in her room in the nurses' quarters. With hope temporarily dampened, Joe turned to his other reason for coming. He gripped the paper bag under his arm. The chocolate bars and cracker jacks in it might help to bridge the enormous gap between himself and the ten-year-old Navaho. The fact was he felt very timid about the visit. What could he think of to say?

The spare, middle-aged woman who was head nurse directed him down a corridor toward the room where he could look for Billie Begay. Then she turned back to a chubby male Navaho interpreter who was trying to explain to an Indian mother that she could not go into the ward with her baby. Joe looked curiously at the baby. It was strapped to a cradleboard, and its dark eyes peered soberly out of what seemed to be far too much covering for a hot afternoon like this.

Just as he reached the door that the nurse had indicated, a ball rolled through it and a crutch poked out in pursuit, almost tripping Joe. He grabbed the rolling ball and then looked into the room. A boy in pajamas, his right leg in a walker type of cast, leaned on one crutch and tried to get the other crutch back under his shoulder.

Maybe this was Billie—Joe wasn't sure he'd recognize the boy. No, Billie wouldn't be up and around three days after a compound fracture.

"Hi," Joe said to the boy on crutches, "I'm looking for Billie Begay."

The youngster pointed to another who was sitting bolt upright in a bed across the room. That was the one he had taxied in, Joe felt sure, in spite of the fact that the boy had a new short haircut and was thoroughly scrubbed. The features were the same—without the knots of pain and fear that had been there when he had first seen them.

"Hi, Billie, how you doin'?"

Billie gave a shy giggle.

The boy on crutches followed part-way across the room. Joe realized he had forgotten to return the ball he'd recovered in the hallway. Winking at the boy on crutches, he turned to Billie.

"Can you catch this if I throw it to you?" he asked, then showed by motions that he was going to toss the ball.

Billie beamed and held out his hands. They were slow in coming together and the ball rolled onto the floor under the bed. Joe had to get down on all fours and reach for it.

"Thank you for bringing in the ball, mister," the one on crutches said. "Nurses won't let us chase things out in the hall."

He and the five other boys in the room, not counting Billie, resumed their circumscribed game of catch.

"Remember me?" Joe asked Billie. "I'm the guy that flew you down here when you broke your leg."

Billie looked cautiously. Then recognition seemed to come.

"Chidi naat'a'i bee?" the child said, obviously asking a question. Then he caught himself and repeated in English, "By airplane?"

"Sure thing, only it's not an airplane. It's a helicopter." Joe couldn't help making the correction. "Look what I brought you."

At the sight of the cracker jack box and chocolate, the circle of pajamaed boys moved closer. Joe realized with dismay that he hadn't brought nearly enough.

Billie clutched the sweets, but he offered no thanks, and Joe thought he looked suspicious. Almost hostile.

"This all you give for bad luck and broken leg?" the boy blurted out almost fiercely. "Greasy Hand say I get horse of my own."

Joe was speechless with confusion for long painful moments. When words returned to him they came with a rush.

"This candy's only a present to show you I'm your friend. I'll bring more presents too. And when we figure out what's right I'll give you something big for your broken leg. But what's this about a horse? And who's Greasy Hand?"

Now it was Billie's turn to be confused. Even if he understood Joe's rapid language, it wasn't easy to decide where to begin a reply. Slowly Joe went over it all again, saying one thing at a time, asking one question at a time. Many of Billie's answers were evasive, or inconclusive, but Joe managed to piece together some kind of picture.

"Washingdoon"—that must be the government—the Indian Service—had long ago taken away all the horses that Billie's family owned, except two. This seemed to be a big crime. Then on top of that, one of the two remaining horses got lost—or something. Now Billie's mother couldn't use the wagon.

Apparently Joe, as a white man, shared some blame for the fact that Billie's family did not have horses. It was only right that he give them a new one to make amends for that earlier crime—and for bringing more bad luck in the form of a broken leg.

The identity of Greasy Hand was a harder knot to untangle, but Joe concluded it must be Manny.

"Is Greasy Hand your uncle?" Joe asked.

Some of the other boys who heard the question giggled. Evidently they understood English and thought he had said something funny. Billie's answer, however, gave him no clue.

"I'm Bitter Root born for Mud," was Billie's incomprehensible comment. "Greasy Hand is Red House, born for Trail-to-Garden."

"What!"

Billie repeated the words.

Under the circumstances Joe could think of nothing to do

but smile. Billie on his part was solemn, aloof. Joe had a strange feeling that the boy had decided this white man was not going to give him the horse after all—the horse that Greasy Hand-Manny had promised he would give.

It was high time to vamoose. "I'll be back to see you again in a couple of days," he said. "And I'll bring candy enough for all the kids."

As Joe turned away from the group, he thought he sensed signs of shy interest in the other boys. But Billie only stared at him coldly.

Puzzled by the riddles Billie had been talking, Joe walked down the corridor. Was Greasy Hand another name for Manny? What business did he have giving Billie the idea that Joe owed him a horse? Where did he really stand with this kid? Maybe Beth Ericson would know the answers.

The head nurse, who had somehow solved the problem of the mother and her baby, now had time enough to answer questions.

"It's Miss Ericson's day off, but the poor girl isn't getting any rest. I'm afraid she's breaking regulations, too. One of the ore-truck drivers came in a little while ago with news that there has been a bad auto accident up near Cove. Some Navahos in a car had a collision with an ore truck. I'm surprised the mine is working today. I'm not sure, but I think Miss Ericson may have driven her car up to the scene of the accident to see what she could do."

"Didn't you send an ambulance?" Joe asked in surprise.

"We aren't equipped to send ambulances way off on emergencies like this," the nurse said a little formally. "It isn't our job."

"Then whose job is it?" A second later Joe wondered why

he was butting into something that was none of his business.

"Nobody's," the head nurse said almost angrily and turned away. "Patients usually have to find their own way of getting in here."

Chapter 9

Joe drove slowly and aimlessly away from the strange assortment of old buildings around the hospital. He passed a precise row of weathered brick houses which had a regimented, military air in spite of the gardens and shrubs around them. Long ago the army had come out this way fighting Indians. Perhaps the army had built the houses. . . .

At the filling station by the bare, silver-colored bridge over the San Juan, he saw an ore truck. It gave him an idea.

Yes, the truck driver knew where the accident had happened. Two minutes later Joe had road directions that would lead to the place and—he hoped—to Beth Ericson. No telling when he'd have another chance to see her and ask his questions about Billie.

Quickly he bought some candy bars and bottled coke and climbed into the jeep. He took just time enough to pour water out of the jeep's water bag onto a newspaper and wrap it around the bottles. Evaporation would keep them cool. Then he sped off in search of Beth and the accident.

At the foot of the mountains he found the road he was looking for. It was steep to begin with and grew rapidly steeper. Good thing he was driving a jeep. He could still make time. It wasn't five yet.

After pulling around a particularly sharp turn, Joe saw a Navaho boy standing beside the road. He stopped to ask directions, and the boy pursed out his lips, indicating more by the motion than by words that he should turn off very soon to the left.

Joe started up again, then took his foot off the accelerator as quickly as he'd put it on. A dozen paces from the boy, lying just beside the road in the hot afternoon sun, was the body of a man. An old Pendleton blanket covered it except for the work shoes, which stuck out.

Killed in the accident, Joe said to himself. Down the bank on the other side of the road lay the smashed-up car.

Just then an old jalopy, filled with Navahos, approached. The driver obviously saw the body, just as he had, but instead of stopping, the car sped on by. Joe caught only a glimpse of the occupants, but he saw that their dark faces were strangely serious.

"What goes on here!" he said out loud. You'd think they—or somebody—would take that poor guy away. He'd tell Beth about the body. She would know what to do about it.

The turn-off to the left was only a faint wagon track, but a car clearly had recently gone up it. Grinding ahead in low, he followed the track. About two hundred yards along he saw a green sedan. He didn't know what kind of car Beth drove, but this had to be hers. Behind it was a hogan with a cluster of Navahos standing or squatting near the door.

Joe leaped out and asked if the nurse was here. No one answered, at first, then a girl said, "In there." She indicated the direction with a nod of her head. Her hair was bobbed and had a wave in it, but she wore the same kind of old-fashioned blouse and big Spanish type of skirt as all the other girls and women.

Now he felt about as silly and confused as he'd ever felt [illegible]is life. He'd started out after Beth, hoping to get some [illegible]ation. And he'd found her in the midst of a lot of troubled people. He couldn't just barge in and start talking as he'd imagined himself doing. And it sure would look funny if he strode nobly on the scene and announced that he'd come to help. Beth would take him for a phony—which he would be. Joe realized that he'd forgotten most of what little first aid he'd learned in the Army. He would just be in the way.

For a long moment he stood embarrassed; then the girl with the bobbed hair came to his rescue. "I'll tell her you're here," she said and disappeared through the door.

The Beth who stepped out of the hogan was not at all the clean, starched-looking girl he'd seen at the hospital. The silly nurse's cap was missing. She had on a mussed blue dress that was smeared around the bottom with red dust. Obviously she'd been kneeling on the ground. And instead of moving with an impersonal, business-like air, she betrayed a kind of child-like surprise—then relief.

"Of all the nice, lucky things," she gasped. "How in the world do you happen to be *here*—right when I need help desperately?"

Joe didn't stop to explain. He asked what he could do.

"Three men need to go to the hospital. One has a broken arm. One seems to have concussion, or maybe a fractured skull. Anyway he hasn't regained consciousness. And one seems to have some busted ribs, plus a few cuts."

Beth stopped to organize her plans. "The man with the broken arm and the one with the ribs are both willing to go to the hospital. But the wife of the man who's unconscious has turned up. She won't let him go. She's sent for a medicine man. Unless the medicine man comes soon and I can persuade him to release his patient, I'll have to go off and leave the poor fellow."

"Where do I come in? Want me to scalp the medicine

man?" The whole business was so grizzly somebody had to say something like that.

Beth stamped her foot in annoyance, but she didn't waste breath telling him what she thought of his sense of humor.

"Did you see anything by the road just below here?" she asked obliquely, then looked at him as if to see how he'd stand up under her test.

"A dead man? Why did they leave him out there?"

Beth gave a little tug on his sleeve and led him over to her car.

"Navahos are terribly afraid of death. You shouldn't even talk about it where they can hear you. They won't touch a corpse if they can help it, because they think the dead man's ghost will do them mischief. Usually they try to get white men to do their burying for them. That's where you come in."

"You mean you want me to bury the guy?" Joe didn't try to show any enthusiasm at this prospect.

"No, silly. But I can't get anybody to go to the hospital if I take that body along too. And it ought to be moved right away. It's been there for hours. From the way these people act I don't think I could get them to help me put the body in the car anyway. . . . So, will you take it away?" she concluded. Her words sounded more like a direction, now, than a request. "I'll tell you where to find a trader who will take care of the burial."

With a feeling of revulsion, Joe looked off toward the place where the abandoned body lay—abandoned, that is, by all except the boy who stood guard, at a safe distance. In Korea he had wondered how the medics could stomach the ·b of bringing in the bodies after a battle.

·alizing that he had betrayed his feelings about the nasty

chore, he hastened to cover up—and over-did it. "Sure, nothing to it. That all you want?"

"Good boy," Beth said earnestly. "You go first. The boy down there understands enough English so that it will be all right. Just tell him he doesn't need to pay you. The man is some kind of uncle or something, and the kid has probably been told to pay white men to bury the body. I'll meet you back at the hospital. Thanks more than I can tell you."

The small, open back end of a jeep is no place to carry a dead Navaho if you want privacy, Joe thought uncomfortably as he moved out onto the highway. There seemed to be an unusual amount of traffic.

After a trader had taken charge of the body, Joe went back to the hospital parking lot to meet Beth. He had waited a few minutes before she fairly sailed out of the hospital door —still in her dusty dress—and paused at the jeep just long enough to say, "Sorry I'm late. The brass in there has been giving me a going-over for doing nurse's work on my own time. You'd think I committed a crime, instead of helping some guys who needed help. I won't be a minute," she called back as she went off again. "As soon as I wash I'm taking you down to the cafe for dinner. You must be starved—and you sure earned a good meal."

She's taking *me!* Joe was a good deal more annoyed than flattered. . . . He'd eat with her all right, but one thing was for sure—he'd grab the check when the waiter put it on the table.

Joe had waited many times for a girl to finish dressing up and he was prepared for the worst. But he'd had time for only one cigarette when Beth appeared.

He stared at her with open surprise. Her summery dress

was a great contrast to the white uniform he somehow had expected.

"That's a pretty fancy get-up just to go and eat at the greasy spoon," he said with a growing sense of self-confidence. "Let's run down to Farmington, where we can eat and maybe dance too."

"That's a nice idea, but some other time. I've got to be back at eleven. I start on night duty tonight."

Great! Trying to have a pleasant evening with a girl who's on night shift! Joe's spirits fell as quickly as they had risen a minute before. This Beth had a way of taking charge of things and running them, and he wasn't sure he liked it. Anyway she hadn't rubbed salt in the wound by suggesting that they use her car.

As he helped her into the jeep he glanced at her again. Look what she had in her hand! A nondescript wind-breaker. Funny girl, this one. She wears a pretty dress, but drags along a beat-up old jacket and insists on eating in a greasy spoon.

Over hot tamales and beans cooked in some Mexican way that Joe didn't like, he and Beth were soon finding out a good deal about each other.

Beth came from Chicago where she'd taken nurse's training. Her father was a railroad man. He'd been sick for a long time while she was in high school. That's how she got interested in nursing.

Joe told about the small ranch on which his father fattened Oklahoma steers for the market.

"You the only kid?" he asked. Somehow he thought she might be. An only child was supposed to have the habit of getting everything its own way.

"Heavens no. I'm the youngest of five. How about you?"

"I've got two younger brothers and a kid sister. The folks, and I guess we boys too, kind of spoil her." Joe grinned as he added the next. "It happens lots of times that way when a girl is the youngest."

"Ouch!" Beth protested. "So you think I'm spoiled." She hesitated, and then went on. "Maybe you're right, but it doesn't seem that way to me. I just know what I want, and I generally get it."

"That's what I mean." Joe smiled at her. He wanted to josh her a little bit, but not enough to make her sore.

"What's wrong with getting what you want, if it doesn't hurt other people—if it helps them?" Beth asked simply.

"What'll you have for dessert?" he asked.

"Fruit salad."

Just like a nurse, he commented inwardly. Ordering something just because it's supposed to be hygienic or healthy.

"Apple pie à la mode for me," he called to the man behind the counter, "fruit salad, and two coffees."

When the food came the counterman left the check, and Joe ostentatiously picked it up.

Beth had made a move for the check too. "Remember, I asked you to dinner. I didn't think you were so old-fashioned that it would bother you. Anyway I'm grateful for what you did this afternoon."

Joe's victory in the matter of the check didn't seem like much of a victory after all—but he had won a point. "It's bad for you to get your way all the time," he said.

"There's some kind of college at Boulder, isn't there?" Beth asked. "Did you go there?"

"I was kind of thinking about going, but I didn't know what I wanted to study. I decided to get some experience first."

"What did you do?" She seemed really interested, so he went on talking about himself—a thing he never found it easy to do unless he was half-kidding.

"I got a job in a garage in Denver. I was just fixing to cut loose and see the country when my draft board caught up with me."

"Is that where you learned to fly a helicopter?"

Joe explained that he hadn't even been in one in the army. "I went to aviation school on the GI bill. That's where I got interested in copters. Already copters are doing a hundred things better than anything else. They can go a lot of places that planes or cars can't go—and in almost any kind of weather. They're the big thing in Alaska, too." Joe was warming up to his subject. "That's one place I want to go."

"It was certainly wonderful that you brought Billie to the hospital in time to prevent infection," Beth said and Joe knew she meant it. "But what's Alaska got that the Reservation hasn't? Roads are so bad here that copters could make all the difference between whether a lot of people lived or died."

"I don't want to be tied down to any one place yet," Joe answered quickly. "There's a lot of the world I haven't seen—and besides, after this prospecting job gives out, there has to be somebody around to pay my wages. From what I've seen that's one thing these Navahos sure couldn't do."

"Isn't it awful?" Beth was quick with sympathy. "They have all this enormous reservation to live on, but they're the poorest people in the whole country."

"What can you expect if they just send sheep where there's not enough grass for prairie dogs? Why don't they do something else—start some businesses or factories or something?" Joe was asking a question that had bothered him.

"They will," Beth said with a confidence Joe couldn't understand. She was planning to spend her whole life on the Reservation and she seemed to feel she could help make a lot of changes around the place. Everything was worked out in her mind: Three years as a hospital nurse in the Indian Service—or in the Public Health Service when it took over the hospital next summer. Then a year away studying public health nursing. Then the rest of her life out in the middle of the Reservation as a field nurse far away from a hospital.

"Nobody's more interested in health than the Navahos." Beth seemed very sure of this. "That's what their religion is all about—no fooling. But when they learn what really causes sickness, and cures it, you watch these people go places. They're very quick to learn."

That was hard for Joe to believe. From the little he'd seen of Navahos he thought they were darn slow at learning. Well, maybe not all of them. Look at Manny.

"You hang around a while and see if I'm not right," Beth said. "I'm only beginning to get acquainted with them and I just plain think they're wonderful. Nobody in the world has more love of living than they do."

Nobody? Joe thought the round-faced girl on the other side of the booth in this third-rate diner had more love of living than anybody he'd ever met. And she obviously enjoyed working—which Joe couldn't figure, in a girl at least. Still, she wasn't like the kids he'd gone with in high school or in the army. He thought of Pat. There was another girl who had a lot of fun, but that was because she'd never worked and would never have to.

"How did you get interested in Indians, or did you just happen to land here?" he asked.

"Dad used to tell me about them some. He worked for the Santa Fe Railroad, and there were Navahos in the section gangs as far east as Chicago. Dad had the *Santa Fe Magazine* around and there was a lot of stuff about them in that. The line runs right through Navaho country down south of here, you know. I didn't just happen to come. I decided to—and here I am."

Beth was here all right, and her presence had an air of dynamic permanence about it.

"Won't you get lonesome, away from home?"

"Sure I miss my family. We had a lot of fun. But I'll go back to see them every year on my vacation. Anyway, I never felt less lonesome. In Chicago there were so many people you never could know any of them very well. Now I'm getting to know other nurses and teachers and Indian Service people—and of course the Navaho patients and their families. I can even talk a little Navaho."

"That reminds me," Joe said. "I sure wish I knew what Billie Begay was talking about this afternoon. He tried to tell me a lot of stuff about 'Washingdoon' taking horses away from his family—"

"Oh, I can explain that," Beth broke in. "The whole Reservation has been overgrazed—too many sheep, too many goats, too many horses. A few years ago the Indian Service saw that it had to protect the land or pretty soon there'd be no grass left at all. So they allowed each family only so many animals. That meant everybody had to give up some sheep or horses or both. Most Navahos hated it, but it really had to be done."

"Sounds reasonable," Joe said. "Another thing, Billie

talked about somebody named Greasy Hand who came to visit him. I've got a hunch I know who it was. Did you happen to see what he looked like?"

"The only visitor I saw was the young long-hair I told you about on the phone. He was a little shorter than you—thin—had a big black hat."

"That must be Manny all right." Joe went on to tell her the strange story about Manny and his disappearance. Beth seemed to make some sense out of it.

"Long hair for young men—even for older men—is out of style in this part of the Reservation where there's been a lot of contact with whites," she said. "I'd never seen a young long-hair until your friend Manny was at the hospital. He must come from some out-of-the-way place, like Navaho Mountain or Monument Valley. Or else he must be plenty sore at the white world—or maybe both. Every once in a while Navahos who have had some education, and have been off the Reservation quite a bit, come back and become more Navaho than ever. I'll bet this Manny is sore at whites or he wouldn't have let his hair grow."

"I don't get it," Joe admitted. Manny had been polite to him.

"I mean he's been turned down for jobs he could do perfectly well—and generally shoved around."

"I still don't get it."

"Well, this is the kind of thing that happens: A couple of weeks ago another girl and I took a trip. We stopped at a diner in Grant's. That's a uranium boomtown off the reservation. While we were eating, a perfectly well-behaved Navaho came in, and they wouldn't serve him. There are plenty of places where Navahos aren't treated the way other people are. A lot of things like that have probably happened to your friend Manny, and they got under his skin."

Beth looked at the clock over the coffee urn. Ten forty-five. She pulled the old windbreaker around her shoulders and stood up. There was just time to change into her uniform and be on the floor by eleven.

She reached the sliding door ahead of Joe and was about to pull it open when she hesitated. Then she let Joe open it, and they stepped out into the cool night.

Chapter 10

Perry decided against flying back to the ranch with Joe to meet his father, who would come down to the claim anyway. They could do all the talking necessary right on the spot. Perry didn't want to waste a day—or even part of a day. In spite of Joe's reminder that it was poor mountaineering practice for a man to go out alone in rough country, Perry was determined to spend one more day on the claim.

So Joe flew him to the cliff and left him there. Perry would have to hitch back to camp the way he had done on the day he made his strike, or else hike all the way. He told Joe to be at the ranch early in the afternoon. Possibly his father would arrive early and want to fly right down.

Back in camp, Joe looked critically at the trailer—something neither he nor Perry had done in two weeks. There was an extra bunk for Mr. Burns—but what a mess! A thick coat of dust lay on and under every spot, except where they had actually slept or sat or eaten.

Better clean up for inspection, the brass is coming, Joe said to himself. About time to muck out anyway. With a zest that amazed him, Joe put some of his army training to work. He made up his bunk and Perry's, and the third bunk too, with all the regulation military folds and tucks. Then with soap and water he scrubbed from ceiling to floor. In such a small place it was amazing how things could get overlooked.

Odd socks, both his and Perry's, lurked in corners. The laundry container was overflowing with smelly clothes. He would fly these back to the ranch.

As he scrubbed and put things away, Joe found a plan developing in his mind. No reason why he shouldn't stop by the hospital and pick up Beth. She might like a ride in the copter. He could take her up as far as Cortez. From there she could go back to the hospital by bus.

He knew she got off duty by seven. Then she would hit the hay. She'd be tired after working all night—and after the long day yesterday. But it ought to be OK to rout her out by one. There would be time enough after that to get to the ranch "by early afternoon." It wouldn't kill Mr. Burns if he had to wait until three, or even later, in case he did arrive ahead of schedule and wanted to fly right on to the camp.

Promptly at one Joe set the copter down in the parking lot by the hospital and went in with a note in his hand. He located a blue-gowned nurse's aide.

"Will you give this note to Miss Ericson, please?" he asked.

The woman was hesitant. "Nobody is supposed to disturb Miss Ericson. She worked all night."

"She'll thank you, and so do I." Joe handed her a silver dollar. The big round coin removed all doubts and the woman disappeared.

She was beaming when she returned. "Miss Ericson said to tell you she was glad I woke her. She'll be right out by your machine."

Before he had time to grow restless, Beth came running around the corner of a building. She had on jeans. That was sensible, Joe thought with pleasure.

She called out, "Do I have to bring anything special?"

"Only whatever you'll need to come back by bus. I can't bring you back."

Beth was as excited as a kid at the circus when she climbed into the cockpit. Right away she had to know about the instruments. They were simple enough to Joe. He was used to them, but he'd be wasting his breath if he tried to explain them all at once. Instead, he made sure her safety belt was fastened, and took off.

As the Canary shuddered and rocked gently, he looked at Beth out of the corner of his eye. Her small hands were clenched into tense little fists—and her eyes were closed. She's scared, he realized, but she's game.

Once up over the tops of the cottonwoods, Joe circled above the town to give Beth a good view. Her eyes were open now and she was looking every way at once. But she sat stiff and motionless—the way you do the first ride on a Ferris wheel when you're afraid you'll rock the bucket.

"Relax," Joe yelled. "We won't tip over."

Beth grinned and leaned forward, still a little cautiously, to look down. They gained some more altitude. "Wonderful . . . wonderful!" She seemed to include the whole Southwest, and this new view of it, and the helicopter—and Joe himself.

"Want to see more?"

Beth's whole glowing presence was enough answer. Joe didn't wait for her words. He sent the Canary into a rapid climb, and enjoyed Beth's intense delight at the grandeur of the unfolding scene below.

"Magnificent! Don't you love this country?" Beth shouted. Her eyes swept from the forested top of the great table land called Mesa Verde in the northeast to the forested summit of the Chuskas off to the southwest. The broken, barren hills and the long stretches of flat land between these two gigantic landmarks were impressive in their own bleak way.

Joe kept below the limit of the copter's altitude in the hot afternoon air and leveled off. He wanted to show Beth what he could make the copter do, not what he couldn't. He made a horseshoe turn, banking steeply up to reverse direction.

"What did you do?" Beth looked bewildered. The scenery was suddenly moving past in the opposite direction.

Ahead and below, at a bend in the full, rushing river, appeared a quiet pool of shoal water. Men and boys were in swimming.

"How's about a swim?" Joe teased her at the top of his voice.

"Can I dive from here?" Beth made as if to unbuckle the safety belt.

This dame might dive in at that. Joe swung quickly away from the river. He was beginning to be prepared for anything from Beth.

Now he headed north toward Cortez. Today was the day to try something he'd wanted to do as long as he'd flown along this route. A tall pinnacle of rock stood out separate from the great mass of Mesa Verde on his right. Without a word he swept toward it, then hovered above its very small summit. Inching down carefully he looked to see if there was a flat space large enough to hold his skids.

There was, he decided, and he aimed for it. Beth sat rigid and gripped the safety belt—the way he fripped his own belt when a dentist was drilling close to a nerve.

"Take it easy. We're all right," he called, wishing he

could spare a hand from the controls to give her a reassuring pat.

Like a wisp of cottonwood fluff settling on the tip of a stiff blade of grass, the Canary came to rest on the pinnacle.

As the whine of the rotor died down, Beth let go of the safety belt and leaned as far forward as she could, then to the side. . . . Space, empty space, going down for hundreds of feet wherever she could see. And not enough room on the sandstone top of the pinnacle for a sure-footed mountain sheep to feel comfortable between the copter and cliff.

"You're good!" Beth finally broke the silence. "How in the world did you do it?"

"Just luck. It was the nearest flat place I could see. We had to land. We're out of gas."

"I've got my mad money," Beth said smiling. "I'll just hop out and walk." She unbuckled the safety belt and started to climb down onto the foot-wide ledge.

"No, you don't!" Joe snapped out fiercely. He grabbed her arm and held her back.

His innards withered in him whenever he saw anyone else near a precipice. He knew for himself what he could do and what he couldn't. But fear shriveled something deep inside him if he saw another person in a dangerous spot.

Beth had won her little victory, but something in her smile told Joe she was sorry for his obvious distress. She settled back in her seat and buckled the belt.

Neither said anything for a while. After Joe's breathing had returned to normal, Beth pointed to the steep sides of Mesa Verde which loomed still higher than the perch on which the copter rested.

"Have you been up there?" she asked.

"Not yet."

"I drove up to the park there a couple of weeks ago. It's a wonderful place. The ruins of the cliff dwellings are fascinating. I want to go back again as soon as I can."

"Maybe I can get some time off and we can go together. Would you like that?"

"I'd love it."

Joe knew her enthusiasm was genuine, and he began to suspect that she found a lot of excitement in life that he had so far missed. . . . One thing was certain. He was going to see a lot more of Beth.

The two were quiet for some time—just looking. A kind of broad valley stretched north and south below them, between Mesa Verde and a big mountain to the west. But it wasn't a real valley. Joe recognized that it was a low gentle pass between two watersheds. The part over which he and Beth had flown was drab. Grayish plants struggled out of red-brown earth. Close up he could have seen occasional magenta or saffron or coral-colored flowers, but from this distance everything was drab—that was the word for it.

Ahead and to the north, however, the land was flecked with green, and in the distance were whole green fields. In that direction lay regular farm houses instead of the hogans they had left behind.

"See the difference?" Joe pointed. "More moisture on the watershed to the north."

"That part," Beth said nodding toward the land where green appeared, "is outside the Reservation." She was right. It was even north of the Ute country. Where the land was greenest, white people owned the farms. Indians lived on the barrens.

"I heard Spencer talking to a fellow from Washington the other day," Joe said. "He claims the Indians don't know how to use their land and it ought to be turned over to whites. He didn't seem to think much of your Indian Service either."

"Why not?"

"I don't know exactly. The general idea was that you pamper the Navahos and that the government ought to get rid of the reservations."

"Look, the Indian Service isn't perfect, but the Navahos would be a whole lot worse off without it. You have to remember that they haven't had a chance to learn all the things that we whites know. When the Reservation was set up, almost a hundred years ago, we signed a treaty promising schools for all the kids. Well, the fact is, eight out of ten Navahos still don't know how to read or write."

"No fooling!" Joe said.

"Just think what they could do with this wonderful country if they were educated! The kids here are just as bright as anywhere, too."

Beth paused.

"We better get going," Joe said with a start. He would be late at the ranch, and he'd catch it but good if old man Burns did happen to arrive early. Still, he took a minute to explain his trick of letting the copter fall off a cliff in hot weather. Then he demonstrated. To Beth the Canary seemed to plummet down, and the face of the sandstone cliff rushed past, almost within arm's reach. But when the machine headed northward again in level flight, she clapped her hands in applause.

Joe wished he could bring Beth down in the middle of the

main street in Cortez. It was broad enough—an amazingly broad street for a small town, or any town. But he didn't dare try a stunt like that.

He landed the Canary, instead, at the edge of town where the highway divided in a great Y.

"That was magnificent!" Beth exclaimed as the noise died down. "It's easy to see why you like being a pilot. I'd give anything to know how. Will you teach me to fly?"

The idea appealed to Joe. Just being with her was fun. Everything—even flying—was more exciting when she was around. But what he said didn't sound that way.

"You'll be a copter pilot when I'm a nurse." Immediately he was sorry he had made the crack. The delight disappeared from Beth's face.

"That was a dumb thing to say," he hurried to explain. "But it's true if you understand what I mean. . . . Let's see your muscle."

He held his fingers on her biceps and asked her to tighten it up. Beth's arm wasn't stringy or soft like some girls'. But it wasn't big either.

"Now feel mine," he said. It didn't take an expert to see that his arms were powerful.

"Superman!" Beth said, mocking him but smiling at the same time. "What is this supposed to prove? That men are superior to women?"

"You got me all wrong, Beth," Joe said in distress. He'd put himself on a spot, but he did have a point. "You could fly a plane all right. Just as well as I can. But it's real exercise to fly a copter for long periods. You have to keep your hands on the controls all the time, and the darn things vibrate. Flying one of these egg-beaters is work."

"And women can't work?"

"Oh, Beth, you know what I mean."

"I'm afraid I do. . . . Didn't you ever go to the circus?"

What was Beth getting at?

"You've seen the girls on the flying trapeze. Well—and what's more—you'd make a very good nurse."

Before he could decide how Beth meant this last remark, she went on, "That reminds me of something I meant to tell you. Billie Begay is going home day after tomorrow."

"You can't tell me you mend broken bones that quick!"

"Of course the bones haven't knit yet. But the danger of infection is over. He'll have a cast on, and he can even get around in it while the bones are knitting."

"Who's going to take him home?"

Beth looked inquiringly at the Canary.

"This copter isn't mine, you know. It was just lucky I had to fly past your place today." Joe felt a little defensive. "Incidentally, the big shot who owns it may be spitting cotton right now because I'm late. Anyway, I'm not sure I can even get time off to pick up the kid in the jeep. Doesn't the hospital have a way?"

"Not if they can help it," Beth said. "They're short of everything."

"That's a fine note. I'll phone you after I see what I can work out."

"Before I came off duty this morning, I told Billie I'd seen you last night. He asked me if you were going to get him a horse. Did you say anything to him about it?" Beth asked cautiously.

"I told you I couldn't figure out exactly what his horse-talk was about. I guess Manny sure enough did put him up to asking me for one," Joe answered. "Manny should have spoken to me about it before he got the kid's hopes up."

"Look at it this way," Beth said carefully. "You told Manny you were sorry you caused the accident, and you wanted to do something to make it right. Manny went to the hospital and did what you asked him to do. He found out Billie's name and he found out Billie needed a horse. As far as Manny was concerned, if you are half-way decent, which he thinks white people aren't, you'll pay damages to Billie by giving him the horse. He just left it to Billie to present his bill."

A bus was turning out of Cortez onto the highway. Beth jumped out of the copter and ran over to the edge of the road to flag it down.

"Thanks again for the ride," she called back. "I don't know when I've had such a good time."

Chapter 11

When he landed Mr. Burns on the cliff above Perry's claim next morning, Joe's mind was still far off on top of the pinnacle near Mesa Verde. The older man's stiff commanding voice might have been on the other side of the mountain, as far as Joe was concerned, while he discussed the day's plans with his son.

Today was a wonderful day, so wonderful that Joe almost missed Mr. Burns' instructions—which meant that it would be even better.

"Pick us up in the jeep about four this afternoon," the boss was saying. "We'll be on the road. Meanwhile, you keep an eye out for the survey crew. I expect them to be looking for our camp sometime after noon."

It took Joe a full minute to realize that he had the morning free. He could sure use the time. He'd go and talk to Brannan the trader about a horse for Billie.

Brannan nodded when Joe entered the store, but he kept on talking in Navaho and trading jokes with an old woman who held her hand in front of her face in a gesture of embarrassment every time she laughed. On the high counter in front of her lay a small hand-woven Navaho rug. Apparently she was trying to decide what she wanted in exchange for it—and also trying to find out what Brannan would give. Once in a while Brannan turned from the woman to one or the other of two men who stood looking over the shelves of groceries. Several times all of them broke into gales of laughter. But no sale of anything was completed so far as Joe could see. After ten minutes or so he began to get restless.

Finally Brannan seemed to feel that he could turn to Joe without offense to his other customers.

"I'd like to buy a horse," Joe said. "Not for myself, but for the Begay kid we talked about the other night. I thought maybe you could help me out. In case I forgot to mention it, it was my fault he broke his leg, and I sort of figured I ought to make up for it."

Real interest shone in Brannan's keen blue eyes. "Word travels fast on the Navaho grapevine," he said. "I knew the day of the accident all about how it happened."

Joe glanced uncomfortably at the Indians who stood near the other end of the counter.

The trader went on, "That Begay family needs another horse, no question. Their wagon hasn't been down here for water since they lost one of their team last winter. Neighbors carry up water for them. And most of their groceries." He paused, then turned back to the Navahos, and said something in their language.

The three talked among themselves for a while. Finally Brannan asked Joe, "How much do you want to pay?"

"Look, I'm new around here. You tell me what horses sell for, then I'll see if I can do anything about it." Joe's hand went to his hip pocket, where he had most of what he'd earned in the last month. He was determined to get a horse, but he didn't want to throw his money away either.

Brannan spoke to the Navahos, who had now been joined

by another woman and a very old man. After a long talk he told Joe he could get something just right for the youngster. "A hundred and twenty-five dollars, with saddle and bridle thrown in."

"That ought to buy a pretty fair horse anywhere," Joe said cautiously. "I thought they might be cheaper around here."

"I can get you one for ten dollars, if you're looking for a bargain in broken wind," the trader said with calculated brutality. "If you want to give the kid a horse that everybody on the mountain knows is good, I can get it for one-twenty-five, saddle and bridle thrown in, and you're lucky to find it. People don't sell good horses just like that."

Joe wasn't going to be outsmarted. Traders were traders anywhere, and he felt sure Brannan would turn a penny for himself somewhere in the deal.

"How much did you lend Billie's mother on that concha belt she pawned?" Joe asked abruptly.

"I think she got ten dollars in credit." Brennan looked with a new interest at Joe, then checked what was written on the tag attached to the belt. "Yeah. Ten dollars."

Joe reached up and felt the weight of the belt. The string of big, ornate conchas was heavy—probably solid silver.

"The metal alone is worth a lot more than ten dollars," Joe said with sudden enjoyment of the bargaining. "Give it back to Billie's mother, and I'll pay you one and a quarter for the horse and trimmings. And if the horse isn't worth it, I'll tell Billie to tell everybody on the moutain you cheated him."

"Don't worry about anybody being cheated," Brannan said with no anger in his voice. "I have to live with these people. If word got around that I was a crook, I wouldn't have a customer." The trader seemed to want to explain himself to Joe. "In case you think I cheated Alaba—that's Billie's mother—you're wrong. Sure, the belt's worth more than ten dollars. I could sell it for maybe sixty or seventy. Look at the workmanship."

Brannan took the belt down and ran his fingers over the designs in the conchas with real admiration. "It was made by one of the best silversmiths at Crownpoint. Alaba came in not long ago and wanted ten dollars' worth of groceries. She offered the belt as a kind of reminder to herself that she owed the money. . . . I haven't sold a piece of pawn in a year. That's the way I work pawn. She'll be glad to see the belt again. It's her whole bank account—and not half as big as her debts."

"I'll give you twenty-five dollars now to show you that I mean business," Joe said to close the deal. "Could you have the horse up at Billie's place day after tomorrow by four in the afternoon? He should be home by then and I'd like to surprise him. I'll be there to pay you the rest. . . . And have the concha belt hanging over the saddle horn. That'll make the surprise even better."

"I'll be up there with the horse," Brannan promised as he took Joe's deposit, "But I don't go for your idea about the belt. You've seen more movies than Alaba has. Just let me hand it to her and explain that you're repaying her for the loss of Billie's help with the sheep. She'll think that's proper."

Beth would think it was proper, too.

Chapter 12

To Joe's immense relief, Mr. Burns had seen enough of Perry's claim at the end of two days. He wanted to go back to the ranch that night, and there was still time.

Singing a tuneless, wordless song of joy that was drowned out by the Canary, Joe headed north. Never before had he been up in such a blaze of sunset colors.

The sky's elation—and Joe's—lingered into the early dusk when he set the copter down at the ranch.

Now for a couple of long-distance calls. "Go right ahead, boy," Spencer boomed expansively and pointed to his office. "No, forget about the charges."

First, Miss Beth Ericson at the Shiprock hospital. He'd hold on till they located her.

Through the open door of the office he could hear Spencer and Burns talking as they settled down in comfortable chairs.

"Perry's strike looks like the real thing," Burns said. "The whole area seems to be worth developing. . . ."

Then Beth was on the wire.

"How's Billie?" He'd better talk so the boss wouldn't be too curious if he overheard.

Beth said Billie would be discharged tomorrow—if anybody came for him.

"Somebody will. I'm leaving here in the morning—about five-thirty."

Beth got the idea. "I knew you'd fix it somehow. Joe, you're wonderful. I'll have Billie ready about six-thirty—right? I can't wait."

That's my girl, Joe thought as he put in his next call to Brannan. It was slow going through.

"Some stupid Indian has staked a claim right in the middle of the piece I want to develop," Burns was saying in the next room.

"Why don't you lease it?" Spencer wanted to know. "You can probably get it cheap."

"I think I can do better than that," Burns answered with a chuckle. "There's not a sign of any development work, which is supposed to be done by the fifteenth of this month. One of my surveyors is ready with a couple of bottles of whiskey to keep the Indian's mind off that claim until after the fifteenth, if he does show up. Which I doubt."

"Can you take the claim over on the fifteenth if there are no improvements?" Spencer asked.

"There might be a little fuss. Some pious Aunt Nelly in the Indian Service could say the fellow has another year, if he wants to renew the claim. But it can be arranged. The AEC wants production now. Still, it's a nuisance. . . ."

Joe was startled. Between Beth and the kid and this horse deal, he hadn't given a thought to Manny the last few days. Now what? Manny was already sore because he thought he'd had a bum deal on the ten-thousand-dollar bonus. But he'd be twice as sore when he found out his claim had been pulled out from under him. Wait a minute—that wasn't all. If Burns got Manny's claim, Manny would be sure to think that Joe Fraser had somehow tricked him. It would look as obvious as two plus two. Manny had told Joe where the claim was, and Joe worked for Burns. So Manny would think he was a heel. He'd sure better straighten things out. But first he had to find the guy.

Before he could worry any more, Brannan answered.

"Joe Fraser speaking—about the horse. Billie is going to want it by seven-thirty tomorrow morning instead of in the afternoon. Could you do him and me a big favor and arrange it?"

This was short notice for Brannan. Maybe the owner of the horse wouldn't be around this evening, but he'd do the best he could.

On the spur of the moment, Joe thought of something else to ask. "Remember that fellow by the same name—the one I mentioned the first time I was in?"

Brannan thought a moment. "You mean somebody named Begay? Oh, yes, Manuelito, wasn't it?"

"Yeah, that's the guy. He been around?"

"No." Brannan seemed a little puzzled, but then he had a suggestion. Every Navaho in the area would be at a squaw dance near his place Friday night. If this Manuelito was around, he'd be there.

"Do you think I could crash the dance?" Joe asked with real interest.

"Why not? I'll be going myself. Want to come along?"

"Can I bring somebody else?"

Brannan laughed and asked if it was a girl.

"That's right," Joe admitted. He hoped Beth would want to go.

"Well, if you've never gone to a squaw dance, you may be surprised. It's not the kind you're used to making a date for."

I bet that trader thinks I'm nuts, Joe thought with amusement. Then he considered what he had said into the phone. If Spencer and Burns had overheard anything, would they get the idea that he had an extracurricular use for the Canary? They certainly couldn't guess he was trying to locate Manny.

"Say, Joe," Spencer remarked cordially as he left the office, "I couldn't help hearing you make some arrangement about a horse. You know you can always use ours when Perry isn't keeping you busy. Nobody around to ride them now anyway. Just tell the wrangler."

"Thanks, Mr. Spencer. I'll tell Manny if I need one." Joe wondered if by any chance Manny had returned to the ranch.

"That no-good Indian took off the other day, the way they all do sooner or later," Spencer said with irritation. "You never can trust an Indian. I've got a new wrangler."

"Thanks again. But the horse I was talking about is for a kid down Shiprock way. I forgot I'd promised to see that he had a ride tomorrow morning. I'd be in real dutch if I didn't deliver. But I got a fellow to fix it up." Whoa—better not say too much.

"Going to try and drag Perry out to a dance?" Burns asked. So he'd overheard something, too.

"I hope he'll go along. Too bad Pat and her friend aren't here so we could take them." Joe felt proud of this touch.

"You tell Perry I said to go. He's been doing a lot of good work and he deserves some relaxation."

Joe kept a straight face. "Will do," he said obligingly as he edged toward the door. "The dance might be a lot of fun."

"Speaking of Indians—" as Joe climbed the stairs to his room Spencer started on a story, "the other day when I was in Gallup . . ."

Joe was curious, but he could hear no more.

CHAPTER 13

By the time Joe had set the Canary down in the parking lot, Billie was swinging toward it on crutches. Beth and another nurse hurried after him, and behind them every window in the hospital was full of curious Navaho patients.

"Hi! You all set, Billie?" Joe asked, but the boy only grinned and proceeded to circle the machine, carefully studying this strange thing that had played such an important part in his life, both for evil and for good. He acted so friendly that Joe was sure Beth had told him he could expect his horse.

"Are you sure it's all right?" the thin, worried-looking nurse asked. "You know where to take the boy?" She seemed to feel that she might be criticized for releasing a patient in such an unorthodox way.

"Don't give it a thought," Joe assured her. "Billie will be home in no time."

"Mr. Fraser is a very careful pilot," Beth said wearily.

Joe caught himself feeling surprised to hear his own last name. But of course she had to be formal on the job. He also suspected that Beth had reassured the other woman on the matter of safety a good many times since he phoned last night. She looked tired, and he wanted to tell her to have a good sleep.

Together they got Billie comfortably stowed in his seat

with the safety belt fastened. And that gave Joe the few seconds he'd been maneuvering for. While the worried nurse examined the belt he managed to say quickly:

"You're off tomorrow night, aren't you? Want to see a squaw dance? Be up at Brannan's trading post about seven tomorrow night. Brannan will take us. There's a chance we'll see Manny. Something's come up. I've got to find him—and I'd like you along."

A smile of warm acceptance came to Beth's face. "OK" was all she said before she began backing away from under the rotor.

Joe started the engine. A cloud of dust rose all around the copter, and he lost sight of Beth until he was up in the air. Then he saw her on the hospital steps waving.

As he approached the clearing around Billie's hogan, Joe looked carefully for any sign of a horse. The boy's mother came to the doorway, but this time she didn't duck inside. She stood watching as the Canary swooped down, hesitated, then settled gently to the earth.

Joe motioned her to stay back until the rotor blades had lost all their momentum. With a keen feeling of disappointment that Brannan had not brought the horse, he unloaded Billie and watched the boy swing across the yard. The two tiny children were frightened by their brother's strange appearance and pulled back desperately on their mother's big skirt when she came forward.

Joe couldn't have guessed that the woman, who had seemed so impassive when he saw her the day of the accident, could be so demonstrative. She hugged Billie joyfully and then got the little ones to join her in laughing at his funny appearance.

Billie said something to his mother—probably about the

horse, for she gave Joe a shy gesture of welcome. Soon he was squatting on the ground near the outdoor fire, drinking coffee and eating fried bread with the family. The coffee was weak and too sweet—Joe suspected the sugar had been boiled in the water together with the grounds. Although the bread was soggy with grease, he ate it and smiled.

But where was Brannan? Maybe it would be best to tell Billie and his mother that the horse should have been here by now. A time or two it occurred to him that the others were listening to something. At last he turned and saw Brannan ride into the clearing, leading a small saddled horse. Joe gave it a quick critical look. A buckskin mare with a black mane and tail and a dark line along the back—a line-back. He knew enough about horses to realize that Brannan had brought a descendant of the mustangs that used to roam the southwest in wild bands. If this pony was true to its breed, Billie would have a horse that was as tough as they come.

Brannan and Alaba Begay passed greetings back and forth in Navaho, then the trader dismounted and looked inquiringly at Joe.

"You tell 'em," Joe said. "You can talk their language."

Brannan squatted down on his heels, cowboy fashion, and after drinking the coffee Alaba offered him, he began to speak in Navaho—sometimes motioning toward Joe, sometimes nodding first toward the Canary and then in the direction of the line-back. Joe studied the pony. She was obviously well trained, for she stood motionless just where Brannan had dropped the reins to the ground. He guessed she was a four year old. With luck Billie could ride her a long time—and he could look forward to colts, too.

At last Brannan paused, as if he had told the full story,

and Billie started to hobble toward his wonderful new possession. A sharp word from Alaba brought the boy to a halt. The horse was looking nervously at this thing with one white, stiff leg and two long yellow sticks. Brannan walked over to the pony and took the reins. Now Billie could move very gradually so the animal would get used to him. He patted the pony, careful not to make any sudden jerky motion with his crutches.

Joe could see what was coming, and it worried him. Billie would try to ride, and the horse might get excited at this strange stiff lot of plaster hanging heavily where a supple leg ought to be.

"Better tell the kid to wait until his leg is well," Joe said to Brannan, and Brannan agreed.

Reluctantly Billie gave up. Then, prompted by his mother, he swung shyly over to Joe and offered a limp little hand.

"Good horse," was all he managed to say before he turned away in embarrassment. His eyes were once more on the buckskin whose reins Brannan had tied to a scraggly pinyon log which made up part of the fence around the sheep corral.

Brannan said something to Alaba and untied a package behind the cantle of his saddle. From it came her belt, and the big silver conchas glistened in the sunlight. She accepted the belt with dignity, then gave a quick smile in Joe's direction. Several of her teeth were gone, but Joe realized now that her features were handsome. She couldn't be very old, either—perhaps not more than twenty-eight.

Giving him one of the quick, limp handshakes to which he was growing accustomed, Alaba said a few words in Navaho. All the while she kept her eyes averted, and at the end she turned away with one hand over her mouth, as if she had been guilty of some bold act that made her feel self-conscious.

"She says she thanks you, and she wants you to know that you have done something that is proper. She had to give a neighbor two lambs to take care of her sheep while Billie was away."

"Will you tell her I'm sorry I have to scram," Joe said to Brannan as he passed him a hundred dollars when no one was looking. "I've got to light out of here. I'm already late to work. . . . See you tomorrow night."

CHAPTER 14

Joe walked around in front of the trading post waiting. When Beth slid out of her car, he said, "Do you know what?"

"No, what?"

"It's good to see you." He studied the tweedy suit she had on. "And you look swell."

"Anyway I'll be warm enough." Beth looked at his sport shirt. "You'll freeze unless you wear a jacket."

"Go along. I've got one."

"I'm dying to hear the mystery about your friend Manny," Beth went right on. "What's come up?"

He told the story about Manny's claim and Burns' plan to get it—and why he felt he had to find Manny, so the guy wouldn't jump to any screwy conclusion that Joe was a low-life.

"I hope we find him," Beth said. It had suddenly become her search too.

Brannan came out now, and they climbed into his station wagon. "Better watch out for Joe here." Brannan smiled broadly and nudged Beth who sat between the two men. "At a squaw dance it's ladies' choice. Some ambitious mother may put her daughter up to dancing with Joe, and if that happens, he'd better dance or have some money ready. The only way a man can shake a partner is to give her a present."

"Lovely idea," Beth said. "Is that why they call it a squaw dance?"

"Well, squaw is a white man's word that Indians mostly don't like, but it has stuck to this ceremony. Even English-speaking Navahos use the name. But it should really be called the girls' dance. It's a kind of coming-out party for Navaho debutantes. Girls and their mothers use it to get a line on likely young bachelors."

"Were you kidding about somebody picking on me?" Joe asked.

"Partly," Brannan answered. "But it sometimes happens to white guys, and it's the honest truth that a man has to pay to get rid of a partner. That's the polite thing to do. It's also polite for a man to pretend he doesn't want to dance. You'll see a lot of them do that. There's a real stag line."

"Guess that's where I'd better look for Manny," Joe said.

"Funny thing about these dances," Brannan went on. "They're about the only ones that whites are allowed to see. From now on until frost comes in the fall there'll be lots of them all over the Reservation. They never start until after the sheep are sheared and the corn is planted. This is the first one around here this summer. It's being given for some draftees who are back home on leave."

"Kind of a Navaho canteen?" Joe suggested.

"That's not the idea. It just happens this one is for GI's. It's really a ceremony used to cleanse any Navaho from the dangerous influence of outsiders—which means mostly whites, of course, these days. The squaw dance itself is only a public and social part of a three-day ceremony called the Enemy Way. It's the old war dance to cleanse warriors who have come in contact with the enemy."

"Seems to be a good place for us to run into trouble," Joe said.

"There won't be any trouble," the trader assured him. "That is, unless a bootlegger has managed to peddle a lot of rot-gut. And the Navaho police will be there to watch out for that."

"What goes on in the part of the ceremony we don't see?" Beth wanted to know.

"It's all performed inside a hogan. Medicine men—Singers, the Navahos call them—chant songs and maybe sprinkle pollen and use prayer sticks. Maybe they even make a painting on the floor with colored sand. I don't know. I've never seen. But just about dusk—that's why we're going now—the Singers come out of the hogan and sing songs for everybody to hear. All night long men will stand in a group and sing. After they've been at it for a while, the dance begins. Don't expect anything spectacular, though. It's about the quietest, slowest kind of dancing you've ever seen."

Brannan switched his headlights on, and the car went up an ungraded wagon track. Clearly it had seen a lot of recent traffic. As he pulled to a halt, Joe exclaimed, "I didn't think there were that many Indians on the whole Reservation."

Pick-up trucks, jalopies, and wagons were arranged in a great circle two and three deep. There seemed to be hundreds of them. And behind the circle of vehicles were saddle horses, tethered singly or in groups. Here and there around the outside of the great circle small fires burned. Seated on the ground around each were family groups. Even in the firelight it was difficult to pick a way among the welter of people and the gear which lay around them. Joe took Beth's arm.

Every few paces the trader stopped to shake hands and

exchange greetings with Navahos. Occasionally he introduced Beth and Joe to some young man, resplendent in cowboy boots and a bright shirt, or to some older man who wore neatly creased trousers which obviously belonged to a business suit. Twice Beth was stopped by people who had been patients in the hospital. But for the most part Joe and Beth just looked about with increasing wonder.

"I never saw so many people with so little noise," Joe whispered after they had reached a kind of branch-covered pavilion where great quantities of stewed mutton and fried bread were being served. There were scores of children everywhere, with hardly a sound out of them, and the grown-ups standing in little knots did their talking in low soft voices. Laughter was the only sharp sound to break through the murmur. Once in a while it would burst out of a group, then die down.

"Aren't they beautiful!" Beth exclaimed eagerly as they passed some women in bright velveteen blouses and equally bright great flowing satin skirts. From their necks hung strings of turquoise beads or necklaces of finely worked silver. Many wore silver concha belts, and one of these was Alaba Begay, who greeted Joe shyly and looked with interest at Beth.

Silver decorations sewed on the women's blouses caught the firelight or flashed as they passed in front of the headlights of a car. Often the bright glint came from the dozens of coins which festooned the sleeves and necks and fronts of the women's blouses.

"All the savings they have in the world are right there on them," Brannan commented. "Wealth means a lot to these people, and they're proud to show it when they can."

"With all that jewelry, they can't be very poor," Joe said

to Beth and the trader when he felt sure they were out of earshot of every Navaho.

"That's what you think," Brannan answered a little brusquely. "A good part of that jewelry was borrowed out of pawn from me or some other trader. It'll be right back in pawn as soon as this shindig is over."

In each group of men, Joe looked intently for the tell-tale knot of long hair which might be Manny's. Only a few of the older men wore buns in the traditional fashion. Manny was nowhere to be seen.

"Here's the best place to watch," Brannan said at last. "Any minute the Singers will come out of that hogan." He pointed to a building off to one side which they could scarcely see in the dim light.

Joe and Beth waited. After what seemed an interminable time, someone lit a huge pile of wood inside the great circle of cars. An imposing old man, who might have modeled for the head on the Indian nickel, stepped out and made an earnest, emotional speech in Navaho. Then a second man spoke, and a third. Each of them obviously had a message that he felt deeply.

There was a gliding kind of sing-song in their voices, broken at intervals by what sounded for all the world like little grunts.

"What are they saying?" Beth finally whispered to Brannan.

"They're telling the young people to respect the old ceremonies and cling to the old ways. And they are saying some uncomplimentary things about Washington—that's the government."

Joe picked out the heavy word "Washingdoon" several times after that.

A drumbeat sounded from the direction of the ceremonial hogan when the speeches drew to a close. Then very slowly a group of men, each with a band of cloth around his head, moved toward the circle, and a chant, some of which was in a high falsetto, filled the air.

Song after song came from the chorus, and occasionally the crowd laughed at the words. To Joe the tunes and words all sounded alike, but the rhythm was tricky. It kept changing and fouling him up as he tried to get the hang of it. It was beyond him to understand how the group of singers could keep their bodies swaying back and forth in a slow tempo that often seemed different from the rhythm of the songs they were singing.

Gradually a large number of young men collected among the pick-ups and in front of them, not far from where Joe and Beth stood. That would be a place to look for Manny.

"It's beginning, I think," Beth whispered. "Look."

A beautifully dressed young girl, with a bright blanket around her shoulders, stood out in the light of the big fire. Moving very slowly with her eyes cast down, she worked her way around behind the group of young men. Soon several other girls followed her. One of them looked familiar. Joe nudged Beth.

"Isn't that the girl who was at the hogan where you took care of those men?"

"Of course! Oh, I want to see what she does."

The girl was deep in the group and she seemed to be tugging on the shirt of a fellow who carefully kept his back turned. The girl was insistent, though. Apparently against his wishes she pulled him by the arm, out into the open, where firelight fell on his face.

"Manny!" Joe exploded—louder than he meant to. He

wanted to run out into the circle, but clearly he would have to wait until the dance was over. Then he would catch Manny as he re-entered the stag line.

The girl now held her blanket partly around Manny's shoulders. Along with other couples in the great circle they began slow, wheeling motions. The men kept turning their backs on the girls as if they were bored, and the girls moved around the men with tiny, unhurried steps. Always they kept their eyes down in modesty.

On and on the dance went. Occasionally a boy reached into his pocket and brought out a coin for his partner, then disappeared into the stag line, where he had to face jokes from his fellows.

But Manny and his partner danced on. Joe grew impatient and moved out in the very front of the crowd to be sure he could head Manny off. He sensed curious, perhaps hostile glances as he shoved ahead. But he didn't care. He had to speak to Manny.

Once as Manny wheeled slowly around he looked up, and Joe knew by the way he turned quickly away that the Navaho had recognized him. Manny said something to the girl who still circled, shyly, sedately around him. And the two of them walked together into the shadows—away from where Joe stood.

There was no telling where to find him now, and Joe was desperate.

"Mr. Brannan," he said in a voice that again was loud for this quiet occasion. "That's the guy I have to see. He went off that way. You've got to help me find him."

"Take it easy, kid," Brannan said soothingly. "Did this fellow see you?"

"Sure he did."

"Then you might as well save your energy," Brannan said with an air of finality. "He must not want to talk to you, and you won't get anywhere playing hide-and-seek here tonight. Just resign yourself to the fact that he's disappeared." Then Brannan added. "It's nearly one. Unless you two want to stay here till dawn and see a lot more of the same we'd better get going."

Reluctantly, Joe agreed to leave.

Nothing had worked out right. He'd scarcely talked to Beth at the dance—too busy watching. Then Manny disappeared like water in the sand. And now Beth was flatly refusing to let Joe drive the jeep ahead of her car even part of the way back to Shiprock.

"I can drive perfectly well alone," she insisted. "Besides you have to get some sleep. You go to work early in the morning, and I have all day to rest."

When Joe tried to follow her anyway in the jeep, she simply pulled off the road and refused to budge until he turned back toward his camp.

"The trouble with you is you're too independent," Joe said crossly. "It's not safe for a girl to be out alone on roads like these at two or three in the morning."

"The trouble with you is you're too conventional. Nothing will happen to me. There's no traffic. Absolutely everybody's at the squaw dance. If anybody leaves early, they'll be going my way. I know how to change tires if I should have a flat—which I won't. My tires are new. If I have engine trouble I'll just wait until somebody comes along."

"Yeah, but you don't know who might come along at this

time of night. You're just a lone girl—and not a very big one." This last really annoyed Beth.

"I know, and you know, who'll come along," she snapped. "Some car full of Navahos. They'll help me." Then she added something that got under his skin, partly because there was no annoyance in her voice as she said it. "I think I know how you feel. You're a little afraid of Navahos, and that's natural. People are often afraid of things they don't understand." She sounded as if he was a little kid and she was old enough to be his mother.

"Well, if that's the way you feel, good night!" Joe stormily backed the jeep to a turning place and drove on to camp.

But when he got to bed he couldn't sleep. What if something did happen to Beth? He'd feel to blame. As far as being afraid of Navahos was concerned, what was Beth getting at anyway? He was afraid for her, not for himself.

He covered the same ground over and over again as he lay in his bunk in the trailer. Then gradually his thoughts turned to Manny.

At six o'clock when the alarm woke Perry, Joe still hadn't gone to sleep, but he'd decided what he was going to do.

He felt irritable and touchy, so he waited until after breakfast before he told Perry what was on his mind—or rather part of what was on his mind.

"Look, Perry," he said. "You're going to be around this claim of yours for some time watching operations start, or else you're going to be prospecting the top of the mountain. There's already a jeep trail cut through to the claim. You're not going to need the copter to get there, and you can't use it to prospect up on the plateau. The jeep will get you to the ranch plenty fast enough whenever you have to go. The fact is you ought to lay me off until some time in October. Then I'll be able to take you up as high as you want to go, or take somebody else up if you're going back to college."

"Dad and I were talking about just that when he was here," Perry said. "The experiment with the copter hasn't worked out very well, through no fault of yours. Dad said he was willing to keep you on—you can do whatever needs doing until we can use the copter again. The truck the surveyors brought up will need looking after, as will the jeep. There will be a lot of trips around for this and that. And you can help me out in the field."

"I appreciate the offer," Joe said. "I'll tell you what I'd like to do, though. I'd like to have two or three weeks off. I'll stow the copter at the ranch before I leave. But right now I want to see some more of this country."

Perry looked at him in a way that reminded Joe of Mr. Burns.

"I know what you're thinking," Joe hastened to say. "You think I've made a uranium strike somewhere and want to go off for a while so I can pretend I made it on my own time. Well, you're wrong. I guarantee I won't file any claim when I come back. I admit I'd like to have a try at prospecting on my own, but I won't do any now. Later if I decide to go off with my own Geiger counter, I'll give you notice so you can get somebody else on this job."

"It's up to you, Joe," Perry said, and his mind was already back on the day's work. He was still checking and rechecking to make sure that his nine-hundred-sixty-acre claim would include any possible uranium-bearing rock in the area.

Joe knew that the surveyor's line would include Manny's claim, too, on the assumption that Manny wouldn't put in his improvements in the ten days' time remaining to him.

"Since it's up to me, what I say is this: I'll fly the copter back to the ranch today, and then light out."

"OK," Perry said. "Have a good trip."

Chapter 15

This is one copter I'll never fly again, Joe thought grimly, as he hauled the Canary into the empty hay barn at the ranch. He used an intricate block-and-tackle rig with a pick-up truck to do the pulling. It was tough to say good-by to the Canary. Joe liked the little machine, but he knew that if he helped Manny to keep his claim, old man Burns would be sore. He'd get another pilot, or sell the copter.

Still, Joe's mind was made up. He had to live with himself the rest of his life, and he'd never feel right if he didn't do his level best to warn Manny. Also, it had come to mean something very important to him to prove to Manny that he wasn't a heel.

If I kept my mouth shut and let Burns get away with this raw deal, I'd be as guilty as he is, Joe thought. Look at it this way. My job goes out the window the minute Burns finds I've messed up his little scheme for getting Manny's claim. But if I keep my nose out of this business, I'll still have my job. My wages will be a kind of pay-off for letting Burns do his dirty work. Burns wouldn't know it, but I would. And that kind of money I don't need. . . . The anger in Joe was strong and steady.

There was even a little anger left over for Beth. He was still sore about the way she had behaved after the squaw dance. Nobody would catch him calling her to see if she got home all right. He could be just as independent as she was.

That afternoon he had no time for banter with the used-car dealer in Cortez.

"What do you expect, a Rolls Royce for seventy-five dollars?" the dealer said cheerfully, after Joe rejected one old car which was newly repainted.

"Don't give me that stuff," Joe snapped. "I don't give a hoot about the paint job. I'm not buying a cracked block."

"Now here's one I just got in, that's . . ."

"Never mind—let me look."

The dealer gave up. He wasn't used to buyers who had only a few dollars to spend and were in a hurry—but who knew how to find out whether a car was in half-way sound condition.

Without wasting time Joe picked out a battered old Chevvy that would run, and that he could pay for. With a few repairs and tuning up it ought to do. Do what? Joe didn't know because he hadn't the remotest idea where Manny was. But he wanted to be able to go anywhere that his search might lead him on the Reservation, which was a mighty rough and big hunk of real estate. About sixteen million acres, he'd heard Perry say.

By Monday noon the car was as reliable as anybody could make it. Joe hadn't asked Spencer if he could stay after putting the copter away. He had just stayed. Now he said good-by, threw his suitcase in the back seat, and drove to Cortez, where he got a carton full of groceries, a water bag, a couple of pans, and two blankets. From there the road led to the Reservation, by way of Shiprock.

As he drove south along the route over which he and Beth

had had their happy flight in the Canary, he began to admit to himself that he felt a deep need to see her, to tell her of his plans. What was the sense of trying to make a big thing out of a quarrel which didn't really amount to much? Maybe he should forget how sore he'd been, and swallow his pride and act as if nothing had happened.

By the time he reached the turn-off to the hospital, the bittersweet temptation grew too great to resist. He went in, only to find that Beth was not there, nor in the nurses' quarters. She had driven off in her car without leaving any word, and she didn't go on duty until eleven at night.

Disappointment, but more than disappointment, shot through Joe as he sat trying to decide what to do. Beth would understand, and approve of, the crazy search he was undertaking. He was certain of that, and he wanted her to know.

Somebody at least ought to know, he realized. No telling where he'd have to go, or how long he'd be gone. He decided to phone his parents—collect. After paying for that horse and then buying a car, he was far from flush.

Joe's father answered the phone. Joe told him exactly what Burns was planning to do about Manny's claim, and explained why he felt he had to start looking in the Navaho haystack for the needle which was Manny. He'd never feel right about it if he didn't warn the guy.

"Good idea, and good luck. Never did have any use for a claim jumper," was all his father said. "Thanks for calling."

Feeling better, he headed away from Shiprock, toward the mountains.

It was a hot walk into Billie Begay's hogan from the last point on the wagon road where he dared to drive the Chevvy.

A wagon could clear those high rocks ahead, but not a car, and a smashed oil pan might ruin his chances of getting to Manny—wherever he was.

Sweating and thirsty he walked into the clearing around Billie's hogan. He had never been a camera fan, but this was one time he wished he could take pictures—moving pictures—in color. Billie, with his cast, sat astride the line-back horse. Tied over the saddle horn were his two crutches. The boy rode slowly behind a flock of sheep, and Alaba, with the two little children skittering around trying to help, was making sure the sheep entered the corral.

Alaba wore her bright blouse and skirt, and the little girl had a long skirt too. Hers reached to the arches of her bare brown feet, and she already seemed to have learned the art of moving gracefully inside the billowing mass of cloth. The little boy had nothing on but an old shirt. His bare brown legs shone like saddle leather in the late sun.

This time Joe would be sure not to scare the horse Billie was riding. He squatted quietly by the small outdoor fire. The little boy was first to spy him after the sheep were all in the corral. In a moment Billie trotted up on the horse with the crutches rattling. His broad smile belied the solemn little voice in which he said, "Hello." Alaba swept toward Joe, her skirt flicking up a little in front and behind with each step. Silently she shook his hand, then motioned for him to resume his seat by the fire.

As she busied herself in the hogan, Joe told Billie why he had come.

"You remember the man you called Greasy Hand?"

Billie nodded.

"I have to see him about something important. Do you know where he is?"

Billie was a complete blank. He hadn't seen the man except that one time at the hospital.

"I don't know," was all he could say.

"Ask your mother," Joe urged, and through Billie as interpreter he gave a description of Manny and of the girl he had danced with at the squaw dance.

"He's a stranger. My mother says ask for the girl at Hosteen Benali's."

It was more than Joe could do to find out who Hosteen Benali was or where this person lived. Brannan would surely know, so he gave up trying.

"You remember you told me Greasy Hand was Red Horse something or other?" Joe asked Billie. "What does that mean?"

"Greasy Hand is Red *House* born for Trail-to-Garden." It all seemed so obvious that Billie couldn't think of anything more to say.

Joe wanted to get away and down to Brannan's, but Alaba filled a cup with coffee. He was glad for something to quench his thirst, although the coffee tasted too weak and too sweet. As soon as he felt he could, he shook hands all around and asked Billie to thank his mother for the coffee.

In his eagerness to find some clue to Manny's whereabouts, Joe had forgotten all about the horse, but Billie reminded him as he started to leave.

Swinging skilfully on his crutches the boy went over to the horse and patted the animal's cheek.

"Good horse," he said.

"What do you call him?" Joe wanted to know.

Billie was puzzled. "My horse."

That kid looks so pleased I'll bet he's glad he broke his

leg, Joe thought, as he hurried down the wagon track toward the Chevvy.

Brannan had closed up the store, but he came to the door of his house when Joe knocked there.

"Sure, I know Hosteen Benali," he said as he led Joe into the living-room, where Navaho rugs lay scattered all around —rugs on the floor, on the sofa, over the backs of chairs, and a big pile of folded ones in the corner. "How come you want to see that old fellow? He doesn't talk a word of English." Brannan asked the question with the inoffensive curiosity of a lonely person to whom the giving and receiving of local gossip is as important and natural as breathing.

"I'm not looking for Benali. I'm looking for a girl who's been staying there—the one who danced with Manny the night of the squaw dance. I still want to find that guy, and I thought she might help me."

"Looking for a Navaho who doesn't want to be found is my idea of a way to waste time," the trader said. "What's so all-fired important about finding this fellow?"

"He thinks I pulled a dirty trick on him, which I didn't. Thought I might as well try to straighten the mess out," Joe explained. He felt cautious about telling any more. If he mentioned the claim, the story might get right back to Perry or his surveyors and cause Manny some extra trouble.

Joe's casual manner seemed to throw Brannan off the scent of any news which might be interesting. He described how to get to the Benali hogan, and Joe realized that this must be the place where he had met Beth the day of the road accident when he had followed her up onto the mountain. Of course, that was the place he'd seen the Navaho girl the first time.

"Is the girl a daughter of this Hosteen Benali?" Joe asked.

"Oh, no. She's just been visiting to help out. Benali's wife is away in a sanatarium, and the girl is some kind of relative of hers. Same clan anyway. She quit a job in a laundry in Gallup to come up here. That's the way these Navahos are, always helping out their relatives. The girl herself comes from over Kayenta way."

"You seem to know everything about the people around here. How do you find out so much?"

"It comes natural. I've lived here for years, and everybody in the neighborhood trades here and talks to me. Most traders are the same way," Brannan said. "But I'll have to admit there are a lot of things I don't know, and the name of that girl at Benali's is one of them. I just realized I haven't heard it—*or* any news about your friend Manuelito."

"What's this clan deal you mentioned? A kind of club?"

"Not a club really, although the members all stick together," Brannan explained. "A clan is a sort of big family group made up of the descendants of one woman ancestor. Navahos think it's very important. When they meet for the first time, they're pretty likely to tell each other what clan they belong to, and what clan they were 'born for'—that's their way of referring to the clans of their fathers."

"Oh, I get it. I couldn't figure out what kind of nonsense the Begay boy was talking. A couple of times he said Manny was 'born for' something or other. Red House born for Trail-to-Garden, I think. I suppose he was talking about these clans then."

"Sure. It means the fellow's mother belongs to the Red

House clan, and that makes him Red House too. His father's a member of the Trail-to-Garden clan."

"Billie's mother said to ask about the girl at Benali's. Maybe the girl and Manny belong to the same clan?"

"Couldn't be," Brannan said. "The girl wouldn't have danced with him if they had been in the same clan."

"Skip it. Don't get me confused," Joe said. Still, there might be a clue in this clan business that would lead to Manny. There had to be a clue somewhere.

"A few clans are spread all over the Reservation," Brannan went on. "I think Red House is one of them. I don't know much about Trail-to-Garden."

"You said something a minute ago I didn't quite get," Joe continued his exploration. "Something about all clans being descended from women. Everybody's descended from women, but you said it as if men didn't count."

"They don't as far as clans are concerned—and a lot of other things, too. Women own the hogans, and often all the sheep. Women really run Navaho affairs, although it looks to white men as if men did."

"Kind of like the squaw dance where the girls choose their partners?"

"A little. A woman can kick a husband out any time she wants to by just putting his saddle outside the hogan. That's a sign for him to vamoose. Women have plenty to say about almost everything."

Joe was silent for a while but then he began to grin. "You know, this gives me an idea. That girl I took to the squaw dance is nuts about Navahos. I bet one reason she likes them is because the women run things."

"Could be," Brannan agreed.

"You know, we had a squabble after the squaw dance. I wanted to drive ahead of her back to Shiprock, because I didn't think it was safe for her to be out alone late at night, but she wouldn't let me. Do you suppose that dance made her feel more independent than usual?"

This didn't seem to Brannan to call for an answer. He got some food out of his refrigerator.

"She seems to have a chip on her shoulder about a lot of things," Joe continued. "She was arguing the other day that the government had broken its promises to give schools to the Navahos."

Brannan put some cheese and crackers on the table and opened two bottles of pop. "She's dead right," he said. "We've kept 'em ignorant and then blamed 'em for being poor. Help yourself."

"Maybe they'd be better off if they weren't tied to the Reservation," Joe said.

Brannan looked at him with a sour smile. "You been hearing some of this 'free-the-Indian' talk?"

"Yeah. It seems to make some sense."

"Let me tell you something, son. First of all, they aren't prisoners on the Reservation. They stay here because it's their home and most of 'em can't make a living anywhere else. This idea about 'freeing' them is so much flapdoodle. The fellows who cooked it up mean that they want to free the land from the Indians. I happen to know that the richest untapped coal beds in the country are in the Reservation. Lots of oil and uranium and other stuff, too."

"Well, why don't they do something about it themselves?" Joe asked.

"Give 'em time, give 'em time. Rome wasn't built in a day."

All this was interesting, but Joe had come to Brannan on specific business. He hadn't got very far in his search for clues about Manny, but he knew his next stop had to be Hosteen Benali's. "If I don't locate Manny through Hosteen Benali, I'm going to cross over the mountains to Lukachukai. I know that's where he stayed last year for a while at least."

"Sounds sensible," Brannan said. "By the way, do you

know what Hosteen means?" Plainly he was trying to keep the conversation going in order to fill as much of the evening as possible.

"Not the slightest idea."

"It means Mister. A good word to use," Brannan advised him. "Too many whites call Navahos by their nicknames, as if they were children."

"I better get going now," Joe said at last.

"What's the hurry? It's only a little way to your trailer and it's not late." Brannan seemed starved for company.

"Oh, I'm not going back there tonight," Joe said. "I'm on vacation. My boss won't be using the copter for a while, so I decided I'd have some fun really camping out."

At this Brannan insisted on putting him up for the night. Later when he finally got to bed, Joe lay a long time thinking. One thing was sure—from now on he'd look for *Hosteen* Manuelito Begay or *Hosteen* Greasy Hand, not Manny.

Chapter 16

Before Joe left in the morning, he got one bit of information Brannan had lacked the night before. The trader discovered from an old woman who came to the store that the girl with the bobbed hair was called Dezbah.

The Chevvy just barely made it to Benali's hogan, but nobody was there. Joe found two other hogans nearby, and outside the first one a woman sat weaving a blanket on a loom. When he spoke she looked frightened, as if she wanted to run and hide.

"I'm looking for Dezbah. Can you tell me where she is?"

The woman hesitated, then indicated the road by pointing with her lips. Dezbah was apparently the only word she understood, and he guessed she was telling him that the girl had gone down the road.

Outside the other hogan was a young woman washing clothes. A little boy played on the ground nearby. This time Joe felt sure his question was understood, although the woman held her hand over her face a long time in the gesture of shyness he had seen so many times now. He waited, and finally she said, "Dezbah has gone home."

"To Kayenta?" Joe asked, remembering Brannan's vague idea that she came from that part of the Reservation.

The woman looked startled, but gave no other indication

that he had made a good guess. Without a word she scurried toward the hogan, shooing the boy ahead of her.

"Is Hosteen Manuelito Begay here?" Joe called after her. He *had* to find out where Manny was. The woman made no sign that she had heard—except that she sped faster toward the hogan. Once inside she closed the door.

She acts as if she thought I was a cop or something, Joe thought with annoyance. But there was clearly no more information to be had here. The woman he had surprised at her weaving had now disappeared, too. Nice friendly people, he thought, bitterly.

What should he do next? Sooner or later he'd find someone at home in Benali's hogan. But he hated to wait around. Better move on across the mountain and go down the other side to Lukachukai. The trading post there was the mail address Manny had put on the claim form he'd left in his cairn.

It was all the Chevvy could do to make it to the top of the pass. Twice the radiator boiled, and he had to get out and add water from his water bag. But the trip down the western side of the mountain was a cinch. He just shifted into low to save the brakes.

All the way down he was surprised at the traffic. He met half a dozen wagons, most of them driven by men and filled with women and children. Flocks of sheep stopped him several times, blatting and trying to go any direction but straight up the narrow road. Behind them rode boys or girls on horseback, singly or in pairs. There were occasional pick-up trucks, too, with kids standing behind the cab or squatting on bundles heaped in the back. A lot of people were moving their belongings and their flocks up onto the mountain.

Joe felt tempted, each time he met a wagon or a rider, to stop and ask about Manny. Once, when he had to turn out at a narrow place to let a lone wagon-driver pass, he talked about the weather and a lot of other things before he popped his question. The man spoke very good English, so there was no doubt that he got the question straight. But he either didn't know anything about Manny or he wouldn't tell. After that one try Joe decided to save his breath until he got to the trading post at Lukachukai.

The road down the mountain followed a canyon, and for a wonder there was a fresh clear stream flowing alongside it. This was the kind of country Joe could go for—it was similar to the mountains west of Boulder. But sagebrush met him when the steep grades approached the plains ahead, and the live stream disappeared in a wash which had torn deeply into the earth. The only sign of water was an occasional mud puddle at the bottom of the wash, and the road across the plain suddenly became dust six inches deep. No wonder people headed up into the mountain.

At the trading post Joe made his inquiry.

"Yes, there was a Manuelito Begay around her a few times about a year ago," the trader said. "But I haven't seen him since. He came from some place over near Monument Valley, I think."

That was news, at least. Manny had never mentioned what part of the country he came from. Joe looked at his Reservation map. Monument Valley was way off in the northwest—north of Kayenta, on the Utah border.

"Monument Valley is farther from a railroad station than any point in the United States," the trader commented. "A hundred and eighty miles or so."

But Joe scarcely heard. . . . Manny and Dezbah came

from the same general area. Dezbah, the woman had said, was going home. Possibly, just possibly, Manny was traveling with her toward his own home. If so, the shortest route lay right through Lukachukai here.

"Did a Navaho girl about seventeen or eighteen—she has bobbed hair—come through here since last Friday night?" Joe asked eagerly. "She might have been with this Manuelito Begay. He's got long hair now."

The trader, like Brannan, looked up in sudden curiosity.

"I have some news for this Manuelito that he'd like to hear. I want to find him," Joe added quickly.

"I don't remember a couple like that, but I don't see everybody. My little girl takes care of the gas pump when I'm busy."

"Would you ask her if she saw two people like I described?"

"She'd know if she did," the trader said. "Can't recall that I ever saw a short-haired girl and a young long-hair together in all the years I've been here. When girls cut their hair, they usually go for young fellows who imitate the whites."

Joe was beginning to feel like a detective, and he was pleased with himself for thinking of the short-hair, long-hair angle. Remembering something else, he added, "The long-hair was probably driving a 'forty-nine Chevrolet pick-up."

"What d'ya know about that!" the trader said after disappearing briefly into his living quarters which adjoined the store. "My little girl did see a couple just like you're looking for. Saturday. They had a Chevrolet pick-up too. She always remembers cars. . . . They stopped for gas. An old woman and young girl were with them."

Joe was excited. He must be on the right trail.

"Did your daughter notice where they were headed?"

"I asked her that. Thought you might want to know, but she didn't pay any attention."

"Fill up my tank," Joe said. "I may need a lot of gas." He was going to work his hunch that the two were Dezbah and Manny, and that they were driving home together, toward Kayenta.

He winced as the meter on the gas pump went higher and higher. How these Navahos could keep their pick-ups on the road with gas so expensive, he couldn't guess. He knew he had to watch his own nickels or he'd be dead broke before he located Manny.

Still, there was one expenditure he had to make. Beth ought to know that he hadn't run out on her the way Manny had run out on him.

"Hiya, Beth," he said when he got her on the phone. "Guess where I am."

Beth couldn't guess. She wasn't even sure who was calling at first, Joe's voice was so faint because of a bad connection.

"I'm over at Lukachukai and I'm headed west. I quit my job for a while. And I'm out looking for that crazy Manny. I decided I had to find him."

Beth said something that sounded friendly, but Joe couldn't hear the exact words.

"See you when I get back." He almost shouted into the phone.

"Good luck," Joe was sure he heard those words before the connection was broken completely. No use trying to get the call through again. He'd said what he had to say, and he wanted to follow his clue without more delay.

"How's the road between here and Kayenta?" He asked the trader.

"Cars have been coming through. You'll be all right if it doesn't rain."

"And what if it does rain?" Joe had more than an academic interest.

"You'll get stuck. But the road usually dries out in about twenty-four hours, except for a few bad spots. Anyway, it's not likely to rain much for the next month or six weeks. Never does. Besides, we've had a drought for the last four years."

Joe looked up at the early afternoon sky. Those were cumulus clouds piled high here and there. They could mean rain, but he guessed the trader must know his weather.

Joe took the road toward Rough Rock, which his map showed was on the way to Kayenta.

Chapter 17

He had been on the road less than ten minutes when he looked back at a turn and saw a cloud of dust behind him. Somebody else was going the same way—and in a hurry.

A few more minutes and there came a wild honking from behind. Joe pulled the Chevvy as far to one side as he dared, and stopped. A jeep—let it pass. It would be good to have one of those high-center, four-wheel-drive affairs instead of the piece of junk he was driving.

But the jeep didn't speed past. It pulled up beside him and stayed there.

Perry, the last person in the world Joe expected to see, emerged from the cloud of dust he'd stirred up. Coughing and sneezing and holding a handkerchief to his face, he stepped over the ruts toward the Chevvy.

What goes on? Joe wondered.

Perry's spasm finally calmed down enough so he could talk, and when he spoke he wasn't the plodding, careful mineralogist. He was the son of old man Burns—and angry.

"What in the name of common sense do you think you're doing?" Perry asked belligerently.

"I might ask what you think you're doing," Joe countered.

"I'm here to persuade you not to try to stir up trouble by finding that Indian."

"Maybe somebody is trying to stir up trouble for him, and

maybe I don't like it," Joe said bristling. Then he thought. How did Perry find out, or guess, that he was looking for Manny? "And what makes you so sure I'm looking for any Indian?"

"Dad told me. The trader Brannan came up this morning with a message for me to call Dad. He'd changed his mind about putting the copter away for the summer. He wanted to use it to send his chief engineer around a lot of places on a quick inspection trip."

Brannan! Joe thought he'd been careful what he said to the trader. But no—this wasn't Brannan's fault.

"Dad was pretty sore when he found the copter was already stored, and he was sore that I didn't know where to find you. He thought maybe your family would know. So he phoned. Your father was very insulting, and he told Dad what you were up to. Brannan told me what direction you'd probably go—and here I am. You didn't get away with it. Dad said you were to return to work immediately."

"Your old man's got a lot of nerve! Tell him for me he can go fly a kite!"

"Joe, what in the world's got into you? Running out on a job and chasing off this way trying to—to cheat us out of a claim. After all we've done for you."

This wasn't Perry talking. Not the Perry he had known. It was Perry trying to speak words his father had put in his mouth. Joe kept quiet to control his anger.

"You and I have always been friends, in spite of everything," Perry spluttered.

Joe struggled to keep his temper, and looked away from Perry. Off to the right of the road was a spectacular line of bluffs. Sandstone. Not long ago he and Perry had climbed the steep sandstone Flatirons near Boulder. They had both loved to try out rock-climbing techniques on those steep slabs. Now it would be fun to scale one of these bluffs with Perry—with the Perry he had grown up with, that is. But Perry's father had thrust a world between them. Maybe the world had always been there, and he hadn't known. But it was sure there now.

"After all we've done for you . . ." Perry's phrase kept tumbling over and over in Joe's mind. As Perry fumed on, he tried to think what the guy could mean.

The Burnses had given him the run of their big house, with its billiard table and rumpus room. He had played tennis on their court, and had beaten Perry, set after endless set—six-two, six-one, six-love. He had had dinner at their home, and he was friends with Mrs. Hathaway, who put food on the table, and with Mrs. Smith, who cooked it. They always let him get a snack from the refrigerator.

Perry had biked out to the ranch often after school, and had gone horseback riding in the days when the Frasers still had horses, and set traps for muskrats in the irrigation ditch. He ate the meals Joe's mother cooked and served. That was the way kids did—traded back and forth with their homes and everything else.

Was there something he had overlooked? He had always paid his own way to the movies when he went with Perry on Friday or Saturday night. He'd taken his turn at treating when they had sodas. He had brought his share of the food on hikes. It had always been fifty-halfty.

Then came the job flying the Canary. Mr. Burns had needed a copter pilot. It was just lucky for him that Joe was around. There weren't many copter pilots available in the whole country.

"We've always done everything we could for you. We even

gave you a job flying our copter." Perry was saying it straight out now. It was the job, but more than that. Apparently the Burnses thought he owed them something because they had allowed him and Perry to be friends.

"And then you try to cheat us out of the best claim in the area. Do you call that loyalty? After all, we've been friends —the best friends." Perry stormed on, repeating himself. He was furious at Joe, but at more than Joe. He was angry at having to meet some test for which he wasn't fully prepared.

Joe still couldn't be sure how much of Perry's anger was his own, and how much was resistance to his father—or an echo of his father. But it didn't make much difference. Perry was trying to play according to a set of rules that didn't make sense to Joe.

"Who's cheating?" Joe finally said. "You and your Dad want a claim that isn't yours. At least he does. He planned to keep Manny drunk if that was necessary to prevent him from working his claim in time. I happen to think that kind of thing is cheating. You hired me and I did my work as long as there was work to do. I don't owe you a thing."

Joe had tried to hold in, but he couldn't help lashing back.

"You mean our friendship doesn't count for anything?" Perry asked in real perplexity. Joe had never seen his usually impassive face so moved. Suddenly he felt sorry—sorry for this agitated kid who didn't understand.

"Sure," Joe leaned out of the car window toward Perry who was standing ankle deep in the dust on the road. "Our friendship has meant a lot to me. But your father didn't buy it, Perry. Anyway, that hasn't anything to do with this business. I happen to think your Dad is playing a lousy trick on Manny, and he won't get by with it, if I can help it."

"Look, Joe," Perry pleaded. "Why should you worry about that Indian? Be realistic. He isn't going to do anything with his claim. None of them do, except maybe to start a piddling little two- or three-man operation. We have a chance for something really big."

"Did you ever think of trying to help Manny make something big of it? You don't even know why he hasn't developed his claim so far. I do."

This line of argument was lost on Perry.

"Don't be ridiculous, Joe. This Indian won't do anything about the claim, unless you stir up trouble. He didn't spend a nickel to locate it, if he's like the other Indian prospectors. Probably he didn't even have a Geiger counter. He just found a piece of yellow rock and had it assayed and is sitting back waiting for millions to roll in. It takes capital to open up a mine like the one we could have with his claim and ours combined."

"Did you ever think of leasing the claim and paying Manny royalties?" Joe asked. Then he added, "Your strike was just as accidental as his, in case you've forgotten—and he made his first."

"But we won't have to spend the money on a lease, unless you spoil things." Perry had come down to the nub of the matter. Money. People weren't loyal, or friends, unless they helped his father, and now him, to make money.

"You can have your job!" Joe burst out. "I'm not coming back until I find Manny."

"Joe, you know this Indian even quit his job at the ranch without so much as giving notice. You can't depend—"

"On an Indian!" Joe finished the sentence for him. It would be hopeless to try to make Perry understand why he felt he had to find Manny.

"It's been nice knowing you," Joe said with heavy sarcasm. And immediately he wondered at his corny words, and regretted them. It hurt him as much as it did Perry, maybe more, to have their friendship go down the drain this way.

Joe had never particularly liked, or disliked, Mr. Burns. Now he hated him—for what he was doing to Manny, and to Perry, and to him.

After Joe had started his car and moved on, he looked in the rear-vision mirror, and Perry was standing there alone in the dust cloud, having another coughing fit.

Chapter 18

On a half-way decent road, Joe figured, he could reach Kayenta by late afternoon, but at this rate it was hard to say how long the journey would take. Every few yards he had to jam on the brakes to keep from snapping a spring, for he couldn't see the chuck holes until he was right on top of them. Fluffy dust filled them almost to the brim. And places that had once been muddy were now mazes of deep ruts cutting in and out of each other, their clay walls sun-baked and hard as brick.

But in spots the road was smooth enough so that Joe could glance away from it. A line of cliffs stretched along on the right, as sudden and final as his break with Perry. Maybe after he had found Manny he would poke around on top of those cliffs looking for uranium. "The stuff is where you find it," the surveyors back at camp were fond of saying. Or he might look around over on Black Mesa, a great stretch of tableland covered with dark trees that stretched on to the left with no apparent end. There was plenty of space for a prospector in this country.

Traffic was light. In the first hour of slow progress Joe met only four vehicles—a covered wagon carrying a whole Navaho family, possibly to the trading post, and three pick-ups. One of these was bright orange with "U.S. Soil Conservation Service" printed on the door. The land around here could sure stand some conservation.

A little later, a sedan as old and battered as his own rattled past. In the back seat was a goat. The Navaho driver waved—all the drivers had waved—and these generous human gestures stood out in contrast to the almost lifeless desolation of the land along the road. But right now Joe valued them doubly. They filled some part of the void left in him by the quarrel with Perry.

Better make time, he suddenly thought. The cottony cumulus clouds had piled up into dark thunderheads without his noticing.

After a long gradual climb he skirted what must be the Round Rock, according to the map. The road began to switch and turn crazily, then to rise and dip down again at a surprising pitch. Joe found he was in about the nastiest piece of landscape he had ever seen. It was as if some poisonous chemical had been poured over the steep little hills all around—like what had happened to the friendship between him and Perry. Not a piece of vegetation survived on the wrinkled, purplish soil, which seemed to go on for miles.

Suddenly with frightening swiftness, the soil turned darker. A recent shower had hit the slope—just enough rainfall to change the surface of the road into grease. He was sliding, almost out of control, and on his right lay a deep gully, just waiting.

Tobogganing down the strange, slick clay, the Chevvy gained speed, and Joe was ready to ram the bank as soon as he could, when the rear wheels took hold. The slide ended as abruptly as it had begun. You could almost draw a pencil line across the road, marking the edge of the area in which rain had fallen.

Farther along, close under the steep, dark slopes of Black Mesa, he found the trading post at Rough Rock. Rough Rock,

Round Rock, Window Rock, Shiprock—the very names in this Navaho country showed what it was like. Shiprock—what was Beth doing now?

He'd been on the road more than three hours since his stop at Lukachukai and had covered less than forty miles—only a little more than half of the distance to Kayenta. Might as well stop here and have a coke.

"How's the road to Kayenta?" Joe asked the trader.

"Which way'd you come?"

Joe told him.

"The road's about the same as you've been over. You can make it if it doesn't rain." All the traders seemed to have the same answer.

"How far is it?"

"Twenty miles. A good long twenty."

Well, he'd try to make it today. If he got into trouble, he could roll up in his blankets and finish the trip in the morning. Then he asked if the trader had seen anything last Saturday of a long-haired man and a short-haired girl in a pick-up—possibly with an older woman and a young girl.

"Sure, they stopped here for cokes. They were headed for Kayenta. They all seemed to live around there."

Joe was jubilant. He was really hot on the trail. Tonight, or tomorrow, he ought to find out in Kayenta just where Manny's home was.

The trader seemed a friendly kind of guy, or else a lonely one. He walked with Joe to the door and looked up at the sky.

"You got chains?" he asked.

"No," Joe admitted. "Why?"

"You might need them. Those clouds don't look good."

Joe felt cautious about all men who had things to sell,

even a friendly-seeming guy like this trader. And he thought of the few five-dollar bills left in his wallet.

"I'll have to try it without chains," he said. "I'm not worried."

"That's up to you. You driven much on reservation roads?"

"Not much," Joe had to admit, but he added "I'm used to bad roads in Colorado."

"They don't have washes in Colorado like we have," the trader said earnestly. "Don't get stuck in one. A flash flood is no joke."

"If it does rain, I'll just stop in my car."

"A flash flood isn't what you may think." The trader evidently wanted to avoid telling Joe he was a greenhorn. But at the same time he wanted to get his point across. "It may not rain at all where you are, but a flash flood can pour down one of those washes from some other place up on the mesa. And when it comes it's like a steam engine, except it doesn't blow a whistle to let you know it's on the way."

"I'll watch out," Joe said, and he meant it. He couldn't explain to this stranger why he didn't dare lose any time. If he lost even a day in warning Manny about his claim, it might be too late to do any good at all. Perry's old man would start pulling wires at 9 A.M., June 16, he was sure of that.

After filling his water bag and checking his oil, he started on the "long twenty miles" to Kayenta.

I'd be there in twenty minutes, if I had a copter, he thought with annoyance. *And* no worry about flash floods. It was pleasant, though, to daydream that copters with superchargers were being mass-produced like cars and were lifting people quickly all over a country which wasn't friendly to autos. He was making a good thing out of it, with a whole string of copters hopping around.

But as he played with the thought Joe kept an eye on the clouds. Tell-tale streamers of dark gray hung down now from huge thunderheads. There must be practically a cloudburst, probably several of them, somewhere up on Black Mesa.

Every time the road dipped into a wash he hesitated at the top of the slope, looked over the bottom of the wash to make sure it was negotiable, and then made a dash for it. He had no intention of getting stuck. Then, several miles out from Rough Rock, he miscalculated. His wheels spun in a puddle half-way across the gully, and, before he could back out, he was in mud up to the hub caps.

His feet sank down as he stepped out of the car. The suction of the soft mud almost pulled off his shoes, but he leaned on the fender and edged his way to dry ground.

Now I see what that trader meant about chains, he grumbled.

Looking around, he realized his wasn't the first car to get into trouble in this wash. Small rocks appeared here and there in the mud. The ends of crushed limbs showed where drivers had chucked sagebrush under wheels to get traction. And somebody must have used a long pole as a lever to help pry a car loose.

Wouldn't hurt at all if I had somebody along to push while I give her the gas.

Joe gave an apprehensive look at the mesa. It was nasty up there. Those ragged streamers still hung low from the clouds. He could hear thunder more clearly, now that the engine wasn't running, and flashes of lightning cut through the sudden dusk which the clouds had brought.

He scrambled onto the bank and began to tear up sage-brush. The plants were tough, and he had to twist and bend to get each branch. First, he tossed some of the stuff down to make a kind of mat to hold him as he chucked other branches under one rear wheel. Then, he repeated the process on the other wheel. When he had made a miniature corduroy road in front of and behind both wheels, he stood up and opened the car door.

The thunder was steady sounding now. Or was it thunder? The roar didn't come and go. . . . In a panic he looked up the wash. Maybe it was a flash flood. The wash was dry as far as he could see, except for its slightly muddy bottom.

Quickly he started the engine and began to rock the Chevvy back and forth. The wheels were catching a little on each backward motion of the car. A heave and they were up out of the hole.

Now for some rocks to fill the hole.

He shut off the engine and as he stepped out he heard the steady thunderous roar again, but terrifyingly loud and close.

Down the wash, almost upon him, came a heaving, lashing wall of water. Joe sprang away and ran stumbling up the steep side of the nearest bank. Before he reached the top, he heard a new crash among the immense roars of the flood. A whole pinyon tree tumbled over and over in water which half-filled the wash where he'd stood a few seconds before. Quivering from the fear that the sudden violence had sent through him, Joe stared around him. In the gloom cast by the heavy storm clouds, all he could see was the tremendous swirl of water below. Not a sign of his car anywhere. Nothing in the dusk to indicate which of the lunging mounds of water in the flood might be caused by the Chevvy.

Suddenly Joe leaped backward. The ground under his feet went limp. When he looked back, the place where he'd been standing had disappeared. He climbed to higher ground. There on a solid outcrop of sandstone he sat down to recover, and to wait.

Rain followed the flood down the mountain, and soon he was drenched. The little pinyons gave no protection against rain like this, which came in great, solid sheets. Joe sat hunched up and miserable on the rock.

Anyway, it couldn't last long, that was certain. And before fifteen minutes passed, the sun was out, appearing with its last afternoon touch of amber.

Everything had happened so fast that Joe half-expected to find the flood too had disappeared, but it was no lower. The thousands of tons of water which had covered the mountainside around him would take time to drain away.

It was nearly dark before the water receded enough for him to see even where the Chevvy was. It stood on its nose, leaning up against the bank fifty feet below where he had left it. The top and rear end were smashed and twisted beyond repair—some big boulder must have done that. A total wreck. Everything in it, food and suitcase and blankets, had been washed away, of course.

Here he was, still wet from the storm, chilly, hungry and afoot. And he'd lost most of what he owned in the world!

It might be hours before the flood would go down enough

for him to cross over and start walking back to Rough Rock. And wouldn't he make a pretty picture coming in and asking for shelter after the trader had warned him?

In the other direction lay Kayenta—perhaps fifteen miles away. If he could keep on the road, and if he didn't run across more washes filled with flash floods, he could make it by one or two in the morning. There was supposed to be a motel in Kayenta where he could get some sleep. He had money enough for that and for a few days' supply of food.

There was only one thing to do and doing it would take him in the direction of Manny. Joe started west while he could still see the road.

The clay was so sticky and slippery that he found it easier to walk at one side of the road, winding in and out among the large clumps of sagebrush which soon took the place of pinyons. Footing was firmer there. But the penetrating darkness of a moonless night came soon, and he had to follow the wheel track again. He felt totally lost just a few feet from it in the high brush.

Not much more than a mile farther along, he heard rushing water ahead. Another wash. That meant he'd have to spend the night where he was.

Chapter 19

Joe moved cautiously in the dark, trying to look through the deep gloom for something—anything—which would serve as shelter from the chilly breeze of the desert night. Twice the sharp points of long stiff yucca leaves jabbed painfully into his shins. There was just no shelter, except the dripping sagebrush, some of which grew tall, reaching almost to his shoulder. With a clump of it as a very porous windbreak, he felt around for a rock or a spot of sod on which to sit, but he could find on the bare earth only the jagged twigs that had dropped off the sagebrush. At least he was lucky that his groping hands didn't brush into a cactus plant. There were probably some around.

Trying to keep warm, Joe paced back and forth in a clear space, whose limits he sensed rather than saw. From time to time he swung his arms across his body, as if in mid-winter. Occasionally he rested squatting on his heels, cowboy fashion. No use to sit anywhere; the damp earth only made him chillier.

Finally he grew so weary he decided he'd have to lie down. Twisting and breaking off branches from the brush, he spread them out to protect himself from the mud. Then he lay down, with his knees curled up to his chest so he could retain as much of his own body heat as possible.

Tough little twigs poked into him, no matter what position he found, and soon his wriggling in search of comfort worked the branches apart, and daubs of mud soaked into his clothes all up and down one side.

The night seemed endless, and when the gold, then crimson of sunrise brought hope of relief, Joe was exhausted and shivering uncontrollably. Hurry, hurry, hurry, he dully commanded the sun, as he plodded in the morning twilight toward the sound of running water ahead.

A strong stream still flowed in the wash, but it was shallow. Probably not more than a foot deep. If he didn't hit quicksand he could easily wade it. Cautiously he looked until he found a place where rocks made riffles in the water. The stream bed would be solid there. He tried, and in four splashing strides he crossed the barrier which had held him up all night.

With any luck a wagon or pick-up might appear on the road before too long. There must be some traffic toward Kayenta from one of the hogans which must lie off somewhere along the wagon trails which occasionally joined the main road. In Kayenta he would rest, and eat. No, he'd eat, then rest. He was hungry, plenty hungry.

For an hour he walked steadily without stopping. The exercise warmed him, although the cool air of night still lingered among the sagebrush. A strong odor of sage began to fill the air, as sunlight struck the gray leaves and rid them of the cover of moisture which had stayed there all night. It might even be pleasant to hike along here after a good night's sleep and a good breakfast.

Joe paused and took a look around. On his left the great bulk of Black Mesa still loomed. In the near distance rippled an apparently endless series of gentle sagebrush hills.

Away off in the distance rose the dim outline of a high butte. That might be the El Capitan he had seen on the map, north and east of Kayenta. He wasn't too far from his goal.

But he was hungry—and thirsty.

A little farther along he saw smoke rising perhaps fifty yards from the road, and he headed for it. Probably a hogan where they would give him water at least.

It turned out to be a queer kind of place. The hogan looked like a hump-backed tepee covered with mud. An entry way faced toward the east, the way all Navaho houses did, but maybe the people belonged to some other tribe. Joe didn't care, so long as they had water to give him.

A small girl, who was not getting very much help from two barking mongrel dogs, was driving sheep away from the corral. In front of the hogan near the fire a woman sat brushing a man's long hair. They all wore the Navaho kind of clothes. Joe hoped that one of them at least could speak English.

"Good morning. Would you please give me a drink of water?"

The man and woman looked up at his voice, and they took his hand politely when he offered it, but Joe was sure they wondered mightily at his mud-smeared clothes.

"I got caught in a flash flood," he said. "The rain . . . it washed my car away. . . ."

The woman, who might have been anywhere between thirty and fifty, said something to the man in what sounded like Navaho. The man smiled and seemed to say a few words of greeting. Then the woman brought a tin cup from inside the house, climbed up into a wagon where the water barrel stood, and reached way down inside. The rain last night didn't put much into that barrel, Joe thought. The water

tasted stale, but it was water, and he accepted the woman's offer of a second cup.

Possibly, just possibly, these people might know something about Manny. "Do you know Hosteen Manuelito Begay?" Joe asked the woman.

She glanced up quickly, then said something to her husband. He answered, without looking at Joe.

"We don't know him," she said. "Why do you want him?"

Joe couldn't explain his complicated reason. She probably

wouldn't understand anyway, so he said rather lamely, "I have to tell him something—important."

"We don't know him."

Joe thanked them for the drink, and said good-by.

He was about to start back toward the road, when he heard a faint call from inside the hogan. It came again and the woman went in.

A moment later she was back, speaking excitedly to her husband.

"Is there something wrong?" Joe asked.

The woman, obviously distressed, ignored him. There seemed to be nothing for Joe to do except leave, and he did so, wondering at the sudden excitement. Perhaps someone was sick. Sickness and accidents seemed to hover around so many of these hogans.

A wagon track led toward the road, and a horse trail crossed it at right angles a little farther along. At their intersection stood a big pile of stones.

A funny place for a cairn, Joe thought—and a funny cairn. Was somebody prospecting this far down off the mountain? He looked toward Black Mesa. The land sloped up gently toward its base, which was at least a mile away—maybe much more. He had learned how deceptive distances could be in the desert air.

The cairn wasn't neatly built, and there was no stake propped up by the rocks in it. Maybe some Navaho who didn't know the regular way had piled this one up. But whoever had done the job had gone to a lot of work. Most of the stones were tiny.

One piece of yellow rock in the pile caught Joe's eye. He picked it up and studied it.

He said out loud in surprise, "Carnotite!"

Maybe he would come back this way, look the country over, and stake out a claim of his own before long. It would be a gesture of independence from the Burnses. He stuck the sample in his pocket and looked around in the pile for claim papers. He found none—only a dozen different kinds of rock, even a few lumps of what looked like turquoise. But the one little piece of carnotite was enough to start him dreaming.

What couldn't he do with a million dollars right now! He'd buy a fleet of copters, and maybe Congress would appropriate money to pay him for taxiing Indian Service people around. Then he'd fly Beth around when she became a field nurse. A copter would be a good ambulance in this country. . . . He and Beth could do a lot of wonderful things if he had a uranium mine. . . .

The sun was really hot now, and Joe realized his feet were getting sore. Light oxfords didn't make the best hiking shoes, and he had begun to wear holes in his socks. Before long he'd have blisters.

Remembering a trick he'd used often in the Rockies, he sat down beside a wash where a little stream still flowed and rested his feet by bathing them in the cool, muddy water.

Now he felt a lot better. Another two hours at the most and he ought to be in Kayenta. But the heat and the dry air made him thirsty again, and he turned off toward the next hogan he saw, perhaps a quarter of a mile from the road.

Near the house he surprised a small boy tending a flock of sheep. The boy took one look at him and ran in terror. Apparently hoping to escape from Joe, he climbed up into the branches of a pinyon. A woman at the hogan saw him coming and dashed into the door, and a man who had been standing beside a horse near the sheep corral hurried after her.

If they're so scared, I'll skip it, Joe decided. I'm not that thirsty. He turned back onto the main road and doggedly kept walking northwest.

It wasn't long before the sound of an engine came from somewhere. He stopped in his tracks and waited. If anybody was going his way, he would hitch a ride or know the reason why.

A mud-splattered panel truck appeared, and Joe began to wave. He guessed by its dark-green color that it belonged to the Indian Service. So much the better. . . . Clanking tire chains slowed, and the truck stopped.

"Can you give me a lift?" Joe asked the Navaho driver.

"What in the world happened to you?" a genial-looking white woman called from the other side of the truck. "Come on, get in."

There was an extra seat behind the driver and Joe slid into it. The woman, who wore some kind of uniform, blue-and-white stripes with an overseas cap, turned around and listened with interest as he told the story of his car and the flash flood.

"We must have got into Rough Rock just after you left yesterday," she said. "I had some shots to give there—I'm a field nurse—and when I was through, it looked so bad that we decided not to try to make it. We stayed at the trading post. That's what you should have done."

"Live and learn," Joe said cheerfully. He really felt cheerful. Now that he had a ride, the loss of his car seemed a long way in the past—and he would be able to eat soon.

Two Navaho women appeared as if by magic out of the sagebrush and the truck stopped.

"You have to get out," the nurse said to Joe, and when she saw his face, she laughed. "Don't worry, I'm not going off and leave you. I'll just give shots to these two women. You can get back in after I'm through."

Joe and the driver climbed out and walked on ahead.

"I'm surprised you could make it across those washes," Joe said to the round-faced, chubby driver. "Have any trouble getting through?"

"I'm used to this road," the driver answered with pride. "I just put on chains and give her the gas. Roads dry out quick after a rain."

Joe had to admit the man was right. Except for occasional puddles in the ruts, the surface of the road seemed almost dry, and it was only noon.

"We didn't start till eleven," the driver went on. "She didn't think it was safe. I could have got through at eight."

"OK, we can go on now," the nurse called. But two minutes later the truck stopped again.

A lean old Navaho, with a red band around his head instead of the usual cowboy hat, stood by the road, holding a long bundle wrapped up in a blanket. He climbed in, sat beside Joe, and laid his bundle with care on the floor of the truck behind him.

"This is Hosteen Yellow Shirt," the nurse said.

The man's face was handsome, alert, and Joe guessed from the deep wrinkles around his eyes and the little puckery lines around his lips that he must be very old.

Soon the old man was talking in Navaho to the driver and laughing. At one point he picked up his bundle, showed it to Joe and said something that both he and the driver thought was particularly funny. When the nurse turned around to speak to Joe, she was laughing, too.

"Hosteen is the leading medicine man around here and he's having a lot of fun at my expense. He's going to treat a patient, and we all think it's a good joke that the white medicine woman—that's me—is giving a lift to a Navaho medicine man."

Joe was amazed. He would have expected hostility between these two. . . . Medicine woman—field nurse—that's what Beth intended to be. She'd be good at it, too.

Before they reached Kayenta, Joe decided that now was the time to tell the full story of his search for Manny. This nurse would understand, and Joe felt sure she would try to get the help of the driver and the old medicine man. He talked fast, adding what he knew about Manny's clan and about Dezbah.

As the truck bumped along, the nurse spoke to the medicine man, partly through the driver as interpreter, partly in Navaho, which she spoke, but apparently not too well.

Finally she turned to Joe and said, "None of us knows your friend, but we think his family may live in Monument Valley. Hosteen Yellow Shirt knows Dezbah. It's not far across country from her place to where we think Hosteen Manuelito lives."

"Which is closer to Kayenta?" Joe wanted to know. He had to decide whether to look up the girl first or Manny.

"There is a good road to Monument Valley. They keep it up for the uranium trucks. You can get there in less than an hour—by car," the nurse said. "You can easily hitch a ride to Gouldings' trading post; then you'll have to get a horse. There's no other way, unless you rent one of Gouldings' special desert jeeps. They can go almost anywhere that a horse can."

It was exasperating, but they made two more stops before

they reached Kayenta, one at a hogan a couple of miles off the road. The nurse stayed in the hogan a long time and then came out smiling. A young girl, not more than sixteen, came out smiling after her. In her arms was a tiny baby.

At last, Joe thought, I've seen a baby that isn't on a cradle board. Wonder what took the nurse so long. Doesn't look like either that girl or the baby is sick.

"I just had to stop there," the nurse said with no apology in her voice. "That girl hasn't been to the clinic for two months and I wanted to find out if she'd had her baby. I wanted her to have it in the hospital, but her mother said no. Apparently things worked out fine. The baby's a beauty."

"Looks like you persuaded her not to use a cradle board," Joe observed.

The nurse laughed. "Wrong guess," she said. "When I came in, she was bathing the baby just the way I had taught her. He'll be on his board again in a minute—and no great harm done either. Except that he should get more of this wonderful sunshine."

Another time Joe would probably have agreed that the sunshine was wonderful, but right now he wasn't interested in it. He wanted to get to Kayenta and food, and then to Monument Valley. At this rate he'd have to wait until tomorrow to hitch a ride.

The other stop was even longer. This hogan was within sight of the main road from Tuba City to Kayenta. The town or village, or whatever Kayenta was, couldn't be more than a mile and a half away. Joe was tempted to get out and walk, but he didn't.

This time the nurse's face was serious when she emerged

from the hogan. Joe wanted to ask her what she had found there, but she obviously didn't want to talk.

Joe thanked her, as she let him out in front of the larger of the two trading posts, then watched the truck bounce away up the street.

He was starved. Nothing to eat all day and the night before. And he was dead tired. He wondered if there was a restaurant or diner, but mostly he wanted a bed now. And *how* he wanted one!

A young white fellow who was pumping gas for a customer pointed out the motel down the road.

"What do they charge?" Joe thought he might as well find out the bad news now.

"Five dollars, I think, for a single."

Joe looked in his wallet and decided he'd forget the restaurant idea. In the trading post, he bought a loaf of bread, a half pound of store cheese, a box of raisins, and a quart of milk. That would fill him up.

As he headed for the door, he heard a booming voice which sounded familiar. Tired and hungry though he was, Joe looked around with interest after the screen door had closed behind him.

"Hi, Mr. Reed!" he called to the big man sitting at the wheel of his car.

"Well! We meet again!" Reed boomed out and extended his hand in a cordial greeting. "Say, you look as if somebody pulled you through a knot hole. And what are you doing here?"

Reed had received his gas and he pulled ahead to make way for a Navaho pick-up which was waiting behind him. When he stopped, Joe told him briefly of his adventure, and then under Reed's questioning he told more fully where he was going—and why.

"If you can wait till tomorrow, I'll give you a lift. I have to go around by Mexican Hat, and Gouldings is on the way."

Did Joe want a lift! He arranged to be in front of the trading post at eight.

The motel had a vacant room, with a bath. When the manager heard that Joe had lost his car and belongings in the flash flood, he turned up with a razor.

Joe's mouth was so full of bread and cheese he could hardly splutter out his thanks for the thoughtful gesture, but it made him feel good. Everything did. He even had enough energy to think of something he ought to do before he took a bath.

He phoned Gouldings to see if anybody there could direct him to Manny's place. Yes, they knew where it was. Was Manny there? They thought so. One more thing: could they rent him a car or a horse so he could get out to Manny's? Their specially equipped desert jeeps would all be in use tomorrow, but they could arrange for a horse. Would it be ready by nine in the morning? Certainly.

Life couldn't be better, Joe thought, as he splashed sleepily in the hot tub—except that I ought to wash the mud off my clothes.

He climbed wearily out and dumped his clothes in the soapy water he had left, then washed them enough to get the worst of the dirt off, hung them up dripping on knobs in the bathroom, and went to bed—with a borrowed alarm clock, set and ticking.

Chapter 20

I'm afraid I have some bad news for you, Fraser," Reed said, before they had gone far the next morning.

Joe's first thought was that Reed couldn't take him as far as Gouldings after all. But that wasn't it.

"Did you monkey with a pile of rocks you found along the road?" Reed asked.

Joe was startled. How did Reed, or anyone, know he had picked up a chunk of carnotite?

"Sure, I ran into a cairn, and look what I found." He fished the specimen out of his wrinkled, but clean blue jeans. "Carnotite. Funny place for a claim, though. It wasn't up on the mountain, and there were no claim papers. . . . And how did *you* know?" This Reed seemed to get around a lot, Joe thought, but it was impossible he could have driven anywhere near that cairn, which was way off the main road, while Joe was there.

"Some Navahos came into Kayenta last night from down that way. Somebody apparently saw you monkeying with that cairn, as you call it, and they're all excited. Don't laugh when I tell you this, but they may make serious trouble for you."

"I'd like to know why! If they're mad about this specimen, I'll return it." Joe's back was up a little. "It's not worth two cents. I figured the prospector didn't want it or he wouldn't have left it."

"Here's what you did. That pile of stones wasn't a prospector's cairn. It was what you might call a good-luck pile. Everybody who passes it always puts a small stone on it for good luck—the way people drop pennies in a wishing well. And you took one of the stones and moved others. Navahos figure that nobody would tamper with a thing like that unless he wanted to bring bad luck."

"What kind of crazy nonsense is that?" Joe began indignantly.

"I remember when I was a kid I heard about somebody swiping a rabbit's foot from some big-league player. He got mad as hops because he thought he needed that rabbit's foot to play good ball. Same idea. But it's a little worse as far as you're concerned. Apparently, right after you visited a hogan in the neighborhood, a woman who had been sick died. Until things calm down, my friend, you are a witch and you caused her death."

Joe was speechless.

"Also, at the next place you visited, a rattlesnake had bitten a lamb. People there already knew you had tampered with the good-luck pile. Therefore, you caused the snake bite, and the lamb died too."

"What!"

"I've been on the Reservation a long time," Reed said, "and I've heard a fair amount about witches. There's a tribal custom that says it's perfectly OK to execute them, and a few people believed to be witches have been killed. You're the first white witch I ever heard of around here, though."

"Are they all nuts?" Joe asked in exasperation. "I didn't

kill the woman who died. I didn't even see her, and I sure don't go around sicking rattlesnakes on lambs. Can't you explain to them?"

"It'll take more than a few words of explaining. You can't just brush off an idea like witchcraft with an explanation that looks reasonable to you. If you don't know what I mean, think back a minute. My ancestors, and maybe yours, believed in witches in Colonial days—executed them, too, at Salem, Massachusetts. Most people are pretty slow to give up old notions about the causes for the troubles they have in this world."

"Yes, but—" Yes but what? Joe couldn't go on.

"You ought to think twice about going out to see that Navaho friend of yours. You see how fast news travels. It's amazing how the grapevine works, but people ride from hogan to hogan, and sometimes the whole Reservation knows about something in just a day or two. Word that you are a witch will reach the country around what's-his-name—Manny's—place before you do. I'll bet five dollars on that. You've advertised all along that you were looking for Manny. If you're a witch, you want to do him some harm. People will protect him, particularly members of his own clan, and they live all through here."

"I couldn't get any information from most of the Navahos at all. That must mean that they thought I was a witch from the beginning," Joe said.

The car was passing some of the most spectacular scenery in the world, but Joe didn't see it, and Reed didn't point it out. Butte after butte towered up all red and gold in the sunlight, lifting flat, inaccessible, unknown tops a thousand feet above the sandy desert floor, but they might not have been there as far as the two men were concerned.

"No, that's different," Reed explained. "You are a white man, and a strange white man. You might even be a policeman of some kind. Navahos have been kicked around a lot by white men, and they think twice before they answer every question you ask. Let me give you a tip. Next time you ask where Manny is, if you decide to go on, ask a Navaho four times. He may say he doesn't know the first three times, but the fourth time he'll tell you the truth. That's just one of their ways. We've got ours, too."

Joe looked at the man in wonder.

"Let me tell you one more thing. It's about Manny, and it may have something to do with the fact that people might have thought you were a policeman. I know where Manny was after he visited the kid in the hospital—and before you saw him at the squaw dance. He was in jail."

Joe was as much startled by this news as by the news that he himself was a witch. He began to suspect that Reed was feeding him a line for some reason—giving him the treatment as a greenhorn.

"You seem to know a mighty lot," he said testily. "How come you didn't tell me all this yesterday."

"I didn't know it yesterday when I saw you. But I thought I might find out something that would help you and your friend Manny, so I got the story about where he'd been. I got it from the Navaho police. You might have thought to check with them yourself before you started on your wild goose chase. For that's what I'm afraid it will turn out to be, at best."

"What's the story?" Joe asked glumly.

Reed pulled the car over to the side of the road and stopped. Ahead was a big sign announcing that Gouldings was off to the left.

"Manny went to Gallup after he visited the hospital. I don't know why he went there—maybe to get supplies for working his claim. But he was there. So was a white man named Spencer, who has a ranch where Manny had a job. Anyway, they met on the street and Spencer began yelling at your friend. Manny got just as sore, and a crowd collected around them. Then Spencer called a cop and claimed Manny was drunk and bothering him and demanded his arrest. It took Manny a couple of days or so to cool down and get his story across, and then the court let him go."

Every new thing Reed said hit Joe harder. He sat with his head in his hands, trying to straighten out the violent tangle in his mind.

"I've piled a lot of stuff on you, Fraser, but I figured you'd take it in the right way. Now I want to give you some advice. You let me take you on to Mexican Hat. I'll see that you get a hitch from there to Shiprock, and you can go back to your job. The world isn't going to come to an end if Manny is rooked on his claim—if it turns out that he is. It'll be a long time before Manny will want anything to do with the white world. He was sore long before you knew him—that's why the long hair. The wonder is that he was off the Reservation at all."

Joe had to have time to think.

"I'll promise you this," Reed went on. "I'll make it my business to see Manny the next time I'm up this way and tell him all you tried to do for him, and what you went through to do it. That'll help him understand that there are whites—and whites—that he's wrong lumping everybody together with guys like Spencer."

The offer was reasonable, Joe realized. But there was one important thing Reed had left out. Joe knew he had to find

Manny for his own sake as well as Manny's. He would feel lousy as long as he lived if he didn't finish this job himself.

"Thanks for what you've told me," he said, "but my mind is made up. I know what I've got to do. I've got to see Manny myself. The best help you can give me is to drive me on in to Gouldings. I should have a horse waiting for me. And you can lend me ten bucks. That car business in the wash kind of set me back on groceries."

Reed shrugged and handed over a twenty-dollar bill. "It's the smallest I've got," he lied, and Joe took it without a word.

As he climbed out of the car in front of Gouldings, Joe turned and said, "If you want to do one more favor, you tell these Navaho police to get on the job and call off any witch-hunters there are around."

"I had a hunch you might not take my advice, and I've already told the police," Reed said grinning. "But this is a big country and they may not get around on time. Just keep your eyes open and don't go monkeying with any strange piles of rock—or anything else you don't understand."

CHAPTER 21

Joe checked over everything in his mind. He had bought a heavy new blanket. That would do if he got caught out, and there was a two-day supply of food wrapped up in it behind the saddle. He had matches. Two canteens of water. And the directions to Manny's hogan. Everything was set, and he swung up onto the pinto pony.

Not until that moment had he glanced at anything around him. As he looked up he felt a sudden tremendous sense of elation. Ahead lay a sweep of desert such as he had never dreamed existed, and plunging upward from it were thin spires of rock and vast mesas—all with cliff walls which must have been eight hundred or a thousand feet straight up and down.

There was not one surprising explosion in the terrain like the Shiprock but dozens of them, and they seemed to rim and make a wall against the kind of world from which he had come. Only the little huddle of buildings at the trading post was an invasion, and these buildings crept for security back against the rocks where two great cliffs met at right angles and protected the tiny foothold of modern life.

The only hints of the outside world he could see ahead of him were the road along which he had come and a landing strip down below him. Suddenly he realized that Reed had driven him up a short steep hill to reach Gouldings, and he hadn't noticed.

He glanced a second time at the landing strip. Sure, you'd want planes in a place like this. Then he remembered he'd heard that copters had been in here a couple of years before, doing surveying. Maybe they'd come again to do prospecting or something. No other way to reach the tops of those buttes or to get around generally. Good as planes were, they didn't carry their landing strips with them, and a copter did. Joe lightly touched the flanks of the pinto and started down the short, steep slope.

The directions he'd been given were simplicity itself. Go south and keep the great butte behind Gouldings on his right. Where the butte ended, go west following wagon tracks. A tall spire in the distance, the Bear's Claw, would be his goal. At the foot of the Bear's Claw was Manny's hogan. He should arrive by late afternoon.

If ever a country looked free of witchhunters, the flat, sandy desert over which Joe rode was it. In most places he could have seen another human being for miles—and he had not seen a soul. The chance that anybody was watching his progress from concealment up on the cliff wall, which he had followed for miles, was about nil. The wall was unscalable for even a short distance without a rope and pitons, the little steel spikes he had learned to use in rock climbing in the Colorado mountains.

By two o'clock the tip of what must be the Bear's Claw stood out very clearly behind a gentle rise in the land. Sagebrush and rabbit bush grew thicker and higher on this hill, but wagons and horses had broken it down so the going was easy for the pinto. Joe was sure a couple of hours at most would bring him to Manny's hogan. But, like any traveler in a strange country, he was glad enough when a rider appeared in the distance coming toward him. Here might be a chance to check on his directions.

The rider held his horse at a steady, slow trot, and it wasn't long before Joe could see that the man kept switching the horse's rump with a short stick the way most Navaho riders seemed to do as a matter of course.

Joe waved as the Navaho approached, and the man soon reined up in front of him.

"Is this the road to the Bear's Claw?" Joe asked when both horses had stopped and stood almost nose to nose, sniffing at each other and seeming to feel as glad as he himself felt at meeting a fellow creature in the vast emptiness of this country. Unlike his horse, the Navaho seemed to take no special interest in meeting someone on the lonely trail. But to Joe's relief he understood English and answered his question.

"This is the road," he said jutting out his lips toward the spire ahead. "Bear's Claw." By now Joe was used to the custom of indicating direction with a nod or a motion of the lips or jaw. He himself would have pointed with a finger, and unconsciously he looked at the man's hands which were both resting on his saddle horn. The little finger and the one next to it on the right hand were missing.

The Navaho seemed in no hurry to move on and Joe decided to offer him a cigarette and try to make some conversation. Perhaps he could get exact instructions about locating Manny's hogan.

The two-fingered man looked startled as Joe held a cigarette toward him in the cross-wise Navaho fashion. And Joe was surprised when the offered cigarette was rejected. However, he asked his question.

"How will I find the hogan of Hosteen Manuelito Begay?"

"Hosteen not at hogan," the man said. "Down in Nakai Canyon looking for horses. Go down there."

The man nodded off to the left and Joe realized for the first time that there was a gap in the landscape in that direction, as if part of the country had suddenly dropped out of sight.

"Maybe Hosteen went long way down canyon to water holes. Find horses there."

This was interesting news. If Joe was to reach Manny, he'd better turn off into the canyon instead of going on to the Bear's Claw.

"I show you how to go down," the man offered, and turned his horse off the wagon trail. Joe followed gratefully and before long he found himself staring into a great gouge in the earth with sides so steep he wondered how anyone could get down into it.

The Navaho led him southward along the rim until a trail appeared, a trail marked with the hoofs of unshod horses. Few of the Navaho ponies Joe had seen were shod. His pinto wasn't, and when he looked at the trail dropping steeply away into the canyon he had a vivid desire for good, strong shoes on the pony—shoes which would catch hold on the sandstone wherever its smooth surface emerged through the sand and rubble.

"Here," the Navaho said, turning his own horse back. "Look by the water holes. Easy to find. Way down."

Switching the rump of his thin chestnut mare, the Navaho disappeared among the low junipers on the canyon rim. Joe sat for a while looking at the jagged emptiness below. It was the reverse of the great buttes along which he had ridden earlier in the day. The canyon was as deep as the buttes were high, and the walls were just as precipitous. But obviously other horsemen had gone down into it, and there would be no chance of missing Manny in that canyon bottom. From here it looked flat and not very broad. The thing to do was to push on. Manny had only six days' time in which to save his claim.

The descent seemed no problem for the nimble pony, and Joe made no attempt to guide the animal, who seemed thoroughly familiar with every switchback. But time and again Joe found himself staring down over the pony's head into sheer space. Heights didn't bother him when he was on foot—or at the controls of a copter. He was sure of his own hands and feet. But a horse was different. One stumble and he'd be a mass of pulp on the rocks far below.

An hour later, though, he breathed easily. The pinto's big unshod hoofs plopped along the fairly solid sand of the canyon bottom. The going was smooth, and the tough pony still seemed fresh enough. Joe ripped off a branch from the first scrub willow he passed and kept touching the pony's rump with it to keep him in a slow trot.

It wasn't long before the animal sped up a little of his own accord, and Joe soon saw why. Ahead at the bottom of a small talus slope, in the otherwise dry stream bed, was a trickle of water. Glad for a chance to stretch his legs and rest, Joe dismounted and let the pony drink. He himself took several good swallows from a canteen and ate a chunk of cheese. Then awkwardly—he was stiff from the unaccustomed hours in the saddle—he started to mount. Just as he put his left foot in the stirrup, a soft, dry whirring sound startled him and the pony.

A rattlesnake! The pony, alarmed, leaped forward.

Joe kept hold of the saddle horn and flung his right leg

up. But his tired muscles betrayed him. His foot, instead of swinging over the pony's rump, struck the nervous animal sharply in the left flank.

Frightened anew by this sudden blow, the pinto heaved up and away—and sent Joe sprawling in the sand.

He was on his feet in an instant, backing away from the sunwarmed heap of broken rock, with just a glimpse of the rattler as it slithered out of sight amid the rubble.

The pinto was in full flight back toward home. The reins, which Joe had knotted together, still hung over the saddle horn. Galloping on the smooth sand, the terrified animal headed straight for the steep trail to the canyon rim.

Joe soon realized that pursuit was futile. He could only go back and wait by the little stream, hoping that the pony might calm down and return there for another drink.

By the time Joe reached the trickle of water again, late afternoon shadows had begun to fill the canyon floor. Fascinated, he watched them push rapidly up the orange-red cliff wall to the east.

Then he looked back through the twilight for the pony. It was nowhere to be seen. His eyes followed the steep trail in all its switchbacks up toward the canyon rim. At last, half-way to the top, he spied the animal.

The pinto had run away for sure. The reins were safely over the saddle horn, so his next stop would be Gouldings. People there would be worried when the riderless horse came in. They'd probably start a search, which wouldn't be necessary because Joe wasn't lost, and, besides, he could surely ride up out of the canyon on one of Manny's horses.

At any rate he was afoot again in strange country without food or blankets. The second time in three days. But now he couldn't be far from the end of his journey. Manny was in the canyon and Joe couldn't miss him. Even if he went hungry, he wouldn't lack for water. There was the trickle here at his feet and the knowledge that water holes lay ahead.

Until the brilliant blue of the sky began to grow first dull, then dark, Joe walked along in the easy gloom of the canyon bottom. But he saw no sign of Manny.

It was so late now that Manny must be waiting until tomorrow to drive his horses to the rim. Joe decided he'd better make himself as comfortable as possible for the night. There was no doubt he could catch Manny in the morning.

The sand of the canyon bottom was a tempting place in which to lie down. For the first part of the night at least it would still be warm, and he could get some sleep. But then he remembered the flash flood. Although no clouds blotted out the early evening stars, he was cautious about the weather in this unpredictable country. He'd feel a lot more comfortable if he were off the canyon bottom. A little farther along he located a mound of rubble at the base of the cliff where chunks of sandstone had scaled off, leaving a shallow cave in the wall.

Up the slope he stumbled slowly. It wasn't much of a climb, but he knew at the top that he was above the reach of any flash flood. No sign of a campfire anywhere in the distance broke through the blackness which now filled the canyon bottom. If Manny was nearby, he must be around a bend.

Joe lit a match to look for a soft spot among the loose stones. He found a place before his first match had burned out, but he was amazed to see that in front of him stood a neat masonry wall. Using more matches, and feeling with his hands, he realized that he was in an ancient cliff dwelling—like the ones at Mesa Verde which he and Beth were going to visit. He could just see how excited Beth would be, discovering a real ancient Indian ruin. . . .

A fire would be a good thing, but there didn't seem to be a stick of wood in the shallow cave. He should have thought to gather some while there was still a little light. There'd be time enough to worry about a fire later on. Right now he was bushed.

Joe stretched out stiffly to get what sleep he could before the chill of the pre-dawn hours drove all warmth out of the canyon.

Chapter 22

Joe was shivering as he took a hasty look around the ruin when it was light enough in the morning. Perhaps a dozen rooms still stood intact, except for their ceilings. Scuffing in the rubble, he realized with disgust that he had missed a bet the night before. The wooden beams which once had held up the ceilings were still here, sticking out of heaps of dried mud and walls which had caved in. He could have had a fire, and he wouldn't have cared last night if he had been burning precious relics out of the past. It had been mighty chilly, but he'd felt too exhausted to search even for brush in the dark. There was no point in a fire now. He'd keep warm by walking. Soon the sun would strike the canyon bottom and then he'd be too warm. It was hotter down here even than up above.

Before he left the ruin, Joe noted with mingled interest and annoyance that the floor of the room farthest back in the shallow niche cave was littered with small corn cobs. A little corn, prepared any way, would taste good right now. He thought with real passion of the food packed in his blanket which the pony had carried off. Then he started out, walking slowly.

Off and on, the tiny stream appeared briefly at one edge or the other of the canyon as it wound its way through apparently endless cliff walls of sandstone. Twice he passed beneath niche caves which apparently held ruins similar to those among which he had spent the night. But he didn't stop to look at them. Finally, he climbed the slope toward a third cave. He was hot now, and tired. The shade there would be welcome.

Where was Manny? Had he possibly driven his horses out at night while Joe slept? It could have happened. When you're chilly and uncomfortable, you feel you haven't closed your eyes all night. The truth is, though, that periods of wakefulness alternate with hours of dead sleep. Why hadn't he thought of that before?

And why was he walking *down* the canyon anyway—why walk at all, if Manny was coming *up* the canyon?

Confusion and something like panic made Joe's head feel light—or was it hunger and the heat? He'd never been so hungry in his life. . . . Pull yourself together, boy, and work out a plan, Joe thought.

There were still six—no, five—days in which to find Manny and get him back to make the improvements on the claim. If Joe was going to wait around for the guy, he ought to do it in a place where he wouldn't starve to death. First, he'd better climb out of this hole and go to Manny's hogan. They'd surely have food there, and Manny would come home in a day or two at least.

As he tried to think calmly and logically, Joe became conscious of a noise which grew rapidly louder.

"A Piper Cub," he said out loud, recognizing the unmistakable sound of the engine. And in a moment a Piper Cub appeared overhead. He wished he was in it, looking for Manny. . . . Wait a minute—what was a plane doing in this desolate place anyway? Maybe it was looking for him. His pony had surely reached home by now, and somebody would be wondering what had happened.

He waved frantically, although the pilot wasn't likely to see him in the deep shade of the cave. Better get out in the sun. He scrambled down the talus slope, but the plane had already disappeared around a bend. Well, if it was on a search mission, it would probably come back this way, and next time he'd be ready to signal it.

In all the years he'd hiked in the mountains, Joe had never been lost, and he knew what a nuisance it was for search parties to look for some tourist who hadn't followed the simple rules of safety. Now here he was—not even lost but probably causing a lot of trouble. All of a sudden he felt embarrassed. But there was nothing he could do about it now. Anyway, the plane could take word back to Gouldings, and there should be a jeep or a horse waiting for him when he climbed out of this hole.

By the time he heard the engine again, Joe had found a

bare, open place on the canyon bottom where the pilot could easily see him. He waved his shirt in a great arc from side to side. As the plane sped by, dangerously low, it dipped its wing. The pilot had seen him. In a few minutes the Cub had climbed up out of the canyon, circled, and made another pass overhead. A long, orange streamer fluttered out and settled onto the sand a hundred yards away. The note attached to it said, "Help coming. Stay where you are."

"Hallelujah, here I come!" Joe began to sing, and echoes from the canyon walls bounced back "Hallelujah!" As long as he'd stirred up this trouble, he had to admit he wouldn't mind a quick, easy way of reaching a square meal. Too bad there wasn't a safe place around where the plane could land. A copter could probably do it in spite of the heat.

The sound of the plane's engine faded over the canyon's east rim, and another sound took its place. Joe's eyes left the sky. A horseman came galloping toward him down the canyon, followed by another horse that was saddled and riderless. Yelling and waving, Joe ran toward them.

The loose horse was startled, but the rider turned and caught its reins. Only when he wheeled around again did Joe realize that the rider was Manny.

"Hey, Manny! You're a sight for sore eyes." And then he realized that Manny was coming *down* the canyon. "So you did go past me last night!"

Manny said absolutely nothing. He just sat in the saddle under his big black hat and looked at Joe.

It was a second before Joe remembered that Manny must be surprised to find him here in this desolate spot.

"I was looking for you," Joe said, feeling confused. All the words he had planned to use when he met Manny had gone shimmering away like the heat waves which rose from the hot sand.

"Are you all right?" Manny asked finally.

"I could use a horse—and about six good hamburgers. Otherwise I'm fine. How about you?" Joe replied.

Manny turned in the saddle, untied the blanket that was behind the cantle, drew out a greasy paper package, and tossed it to Joe. Navaho fried bread. Without any ceremony Joe filled his mouth. He was ravenous.

As Joe ate, Manny dismounted and led the horses to the tiny stream in the canyon bed.

A strange silence hung between the two of them, and when the horses had drunk a little water, Manny led them back and wordlessly nodded toward the extra one. Then he glanced up at the sun and nodded at Joe a second time as if to say, "Hurry. We have no time to lose."

"Manny, I've got a lot of things I want to tell you," Joe said after he was in the saddle. He shifted uncomfortably—he was sore from yesterday's ride. "I came out here looking for you—but how did you happen along right now with an extra horse?"

"I heard yesterday that somebody like you was looking for me. This morning I heard that Two Fingers gave you wrong directions. So I came."

Manny smiled the way he had when they worked on the copter together back at the ranch. Apparently he felt good about finding Joe. This would make it easier for Joe to explain why he had come. But first he had some more questions.

"Did you see my horse? Is that why you brought one for me to ride?" he asked.

Now it was Manny's turn to be puzzled. "I thought maybe

your horse was sick. There's poison water in this canyon. It might kill your horse. You too."

"What!" Joe had felt lousy—tired and dizzy. Maybe it wasn't just heat and hunger and weariness. "I've been drinking this water!"

"Where?"

Joe pointed to the stream bed where the trickle appeared and disappeared.

"That's all?"

What was Manny getting at?

"Did you drink from the water holes down below?"

"No. Why?"

"This water is good," Manny said as if some weight had been lifted from him. "But the water holes down below have something in them that makes horses, and people, die. Did your horse drink there?"

"I didn't get that far," Joe said. But the pinto was no longer on his mind. He thought back quickly, trying to put things together.

Joe thought: Two Fingers sent me down here into the canyon. He told me to look for Manny near the water holes—told me more than once. But he knew all the time that Manny wasn't here. He knew the water holes were poison—and he thought I'd drink from them.

The picture of what Two Fingers had tried to do sent a flash flood of anger through Joe. When he calmed down a little, he added one more piece to the puzzle-picture he had put together. Two Fingers had tried to murder him because he thought Joe was a witch!

Reed had warned him he might get into trouble. Reed even mentioned that Navahos had been known to execute witches. But—but better not jump to conclusions.

"Did Two Fingers know the water was bad? Did he know you weren't down here? Why did he send me this way?" Joe piled the questions one on top of another.

The only sound from Manny's direction was the squeak of his saddle and the plop-plop of his horse's hoofs in the sand. Manny had withdrawn into himself. It was true. Two Fingers *had* tried to kill him for being a witch!

"Manny, did he think I was a witch?"

Manny looked up studying Joe's face. "Why did you say that?" he asked.

Joe told him the whole story of losing his car, lifting the carnotite from the good-luck pile, then hearing from Reed of the bad luck he was supposed to have caused. The carnotite specimen was still in his pocket, and he showed it to Manny.

"I may be a fool, but I'm not a witch," Joe concluded. "You believe that, don't you?"

"Why did you follow me?" Manny asked. There was no friendliness in his voice now. "Did Spencer send you, or the police?"

"Look, Manny. We've got a lot of things to straighten out," Joe said. He realized now, much more than he had in the beginning, how deeply Manny must distrust Spencer and anyone to whom Spencer seemed friendly—in fact, how deeply Manny distrusted all whites.

"Spencer didn't send me," Joe said bluntly. "And I'm no cop. I despise Spencer as much as you do. I heard about the lousy deal he gave you in Gallup. But I didn't come all the way out here to tell you that. I didn't even know about the Gallup business when I started."

The going was still easy for the horses, but Joe wished he could sit down with Manny and talk out the whole complicated mess. Still, that might take a long time, and it would be no joke to climb up the steep trail after dark. He'd do the best he could in the saddle, riding alongside.

"I wanted to see you for several reasons," Joe said. "But I was in a hurry on account of one particular thing."

Manny said nothing, and the look on his face was detached as Joe explained what he had found out about the ten-thousand-dollar bonus: that Manny had no special cause to be more angry about it than a hundred other men, white as well as Navaho, who had been misled by it.

"Sure it's a cheap run-around," Joe said. "But it doesn't prove that all white men give Navahos a raw deal. Only some of them. Spencer's one. I didn't know that at first. So is Perry's father—and I guess Perry, too." Joe said this last reluctantly, but after the row he'd had with Perry on the road from Lukachukai, that was the only thing he could say.

"I chased after you in a hurry because of Perry's father," Joe went on, knowing that he wasn't telling his story in an orderly way as he had planned. "Perry's father is going to take your claim unless you make your improvements in the next five days. Perry has tested the ore, and it's good stuff—very good in fact. You already know that. And old man Burns wants to get it away from you. He figures—" Joe hated to say it, but he wanted to make Manny mad, "you're just a dumb Indian and you won't know what to do to protect your rights. He found out I was looking for you to remind you about making improvements, and he sent Perry on my trail to try and stop me."

Manny rode silently and Joe wondered what thoughts were working in his mind, hidden by his serious face and by a philosophy Joe could only dimly guess at.

"I don't like to see guys get cheated. And I don't like to have anybody think I helped with the cheating." Joe looked straight at Manny. "You did think I was fixing to rook you out of your claim and help Burns to get it, didn't you? You told me where the claim was. You found Perry had a claim at just about the same place. You must have thought I led Perry to your claim. I worked for him, so why wouldn't I?"

Joe knew from the way Manny dropped his eyes that he had guessed right, and he went on, "It just happens that I didn't tell Perry a thing about your claim. He didn't even recognize your name on the claim papers."

Manny had been switching his horse lightly every few steps, Navaho fashion. The hand that held the switch hung poised while the horse walked on. That was the only sign that he had heard.

"I'll go back with you and help you make your improvements. Two days' work or even a day's. Opening a shaft or clearing a road will be enough to count as improvements. And if we start back tomorrow we'll have time."

The whole problem didn't seem that simple to Manny, but at least he spoke.

"Why should I go back? Even if I get the claim, what good is it? Burns or some other white man will cheat me out of it later. I have no money to mine it myself. I'm sorry I ever found the yellow rock. It just gives white men one more thing to steal from me and my people. I'm going to stay here with my own people. I will live from my sheep as Navahos have always done—and white men won't come here."

"I came here. Other white men will come. And some of them are going to bring along things that can do you some good. Your people can't just go on raising sheep and doing nothing else. There are more and more Navahos and less and less grass for your sheep."

"My people were happy until the white man came," Manny said defiantly.

"Maybe they were. But look, Manny, you've got a pick-up truck, for instance. Don't give me this stuff about sheep. There's nothing wrong with pick-ups and cars. Your people need them to get around. They use them, and you're a good mechanic. You could work on planes and copters, and lots of them are needed here. You could easy be a pilot. Look at Billie Begay. He might be dead now if I hadn't had a copter to take him to the hospital."

Joe was sorry he'd mentioned Billie. He knew Manny could say that Billie wouldn't have needed to go to the hospital if it hadn't been for a copter.

"Billie got his horse—a good young line-back mare," Joe hurried to say. "The hospital did a fine job on his leg. He'll be as good as new in a few weeks. A lot more hospitals would help your people. You saw in the army what doctors can do to make people well—and you Navahos can get rich enough to have all the hospitals and everything else you want. Just don't be stubborn about it."

"How?" Manny's one word was not so much a question as a statement of utter disbelief that his people could ever be rich.

Joe stopped his horse and by so doing forced Manny to stop. They had nearly reached the trail up to the canyon rim. Joe looked at the gigantic rock walls.

"What happens to the rain here? It hits the land and then goes down this canyon and that's the last of it. I'm no engineer, but I'll bet if there was a dam across this canyon, there would be enough water from the rain and snow so you could have a lake here all year round. The water could turn Monument Valley into farm land. Navahos could build the dam and grow the crops."

"I'm not a farmer," Manny said stubbornly.

"Oh, all right. Then you people could mine the coal that lies under your reservation. Brannan told me there is a lot of it. And coal could run power stations. You could have lights in your houses, and factories to work in."

Manny's reply to that was quick and bitter. "The whites will have the factories and the Navahos will do the work."

"There are plenty of whites who don't have factories. Me for one." Joe was beginning to enjoy the argument. "But there's no law that says Navahos can't have their own factories and dams—and everything. You and guys like you who know about machinery could teach the others."

"My people don't want factories. They want sheep." Manny said this as if it were the final word and turned his horse toward the steep trail up the canyon side.

Desperately Joe thought about the claim again. Manny must not be allowed to throw it away. As the horses started forward single file, he called ahead, "If you go back with me and improve your claim, you can lease it and get thousands of dollars to buy sheep—or whatever you want."

Manny didn't even look around. Joe stared at the back of the domed black hat. He was half angry and half ready to laugh at his own foolishness. Twice he'd almost got killed, just to hear this guy say he wanted nothing but a flock of blatting sheep. No, that wasn't fair. Manny was only using sheep in place of something else, something Joe didn't know how to argue about.

They had gone only a few yards up the trail when two Navaho horsemen trotted out from behind some rocks just below them. Joe learned through Manny that they, too, were searching for him.

They had been sent from Gouldings. "Manny," Joe said, "please tell them I appreciate it. I'm sorry I caused all this trouble."

There could be no more talk now. All four horses began struggling up toward the canyon rim.

Chapter 23

An excited voice called, "Joe," as his weary horse heaved him up over the canyon rim. "Joe!" The voice came from the direction of a jeep that stood not far away.

"Beth!" Joe called back hoarsely—too surprised to be puzzled by her presence.

Stiffly he dismounted and waited while Beth ran toward him.

"Joe, are you all right?"

Behind Beth a big figure ambled across the sand. Reed!

Joe broke into laughter which was almost hysterical. First Manny had appeared as if by magic, then Beth, and now Reed.

When he recovered enough to speak he asked, "How come? How come you two guys are here?"

Before anyone could answer, Beth ran back to the car, and Joe found himself shaking hands with Reed and introducing Manny.

Reluctantly, it seemed to Joe, Manny dismounted, while the two other Navaho riders sat relaxed in the saddle a little way off resting their horses.

"Anybody want a coke?" Beth called, pulling the bottles out from under damp newspapers. Then she added something slowly in Navaho, and looked for reassurance toward Reed.

Reed smiled and spoke to the two men who were holding themselves aloof.

"Come on," Beth said. "Refreshments." And everyone moved toward the jeep. She had sandwiches as well as cokes. By common consent the sandwiches were left for Joe.

Between bites he repeated his question, "How come you guys are here?"

"First tell us about you. Are you really all right?" Beth insisted.

Joe waited a minute while he swallowed. "Nothing wrong with me that more of this won't cure." He unwrapped a second sandwich. "Come on, give with the story while I eat."

"You tell him, Mr. Reed," Beth said.

The two riders, still in the saddle, said something to Manny, waved to Joe, and then trotted off among the junipers.

"Let's see," Reed began. "After I left Gouldings I went to Mexican Hat. I don't mind admitting I was worried about you. Last night I phoned the Navaho Police from Mexican Hat to see if everything was under control."

"How would they know?" Joe asked. "I only saw one person yesterday after I left Gouldings. Or did they find out about my horse? It ran away, in case you don't know."

"That's it," said Reed. "Your pony came back alone to its owner's hogan near Gouldings. He was worried and rode into Gouldings with the news. They got these two men to follow your trail, and they phoned the Navaho police. The police ordered out a Navaho Civil Air Patrol plane to search for you this morning. I didn't want to miss the fun, so I came over from Mexican Hat to Gouldings a little while ago. There I met this determined young lady."

"Tell him about the poison water holes," Beth interrupted. "Joe, I was afraid—"

She stopped abruptly, and Joe sensed it was on account of Manny. "We know about that," Joe said. "But how did you find out?"

"It seems the man who sent you down into Nakai Canyon is something of a braggart as well as an ingenious witch-hunter," Reed said. "He told somebody, who told somebody who told somebody else. Anyway word got to the Navaho police, and they told me."

"Wish I could have seen the excitement, instead of causing it," Joe said. He had finished a banana. Beth must have brought it all the way from Shiprock. The only fresh fruit he'd seen in any trading post was oranges.

"Now, Joe, you tell us what happened," Beth said. "I can't wait."

"Give a guy a chance." Joe bit into a chocolate bar Beth had given him along with the banana. "You go first."

"Well, I turned my radio on at seven this morning after I came off duty. Almost the first thing I heard was the Gallup announcer saying that the Navaho Civil Air Patrol—and I don't know who else—had been ordered out to search for you. You'd disappeared in the direction of Nakai Canyon and your horse had returned without you. I got another nurse to take over my duty tonight and started out. Most of the road around through Dennehotso had just been graded so I made good time. Then Mr. Reed offered me a ride in one of the Gouldings' desert jeeps. And here I am."

"Let's sit down on something soft,—like a car seat,"

Joe said. He had been standing as he ate. His legs were too stiff and sore for him to squat, and there were no sandstone outcroppings, chair-high, around handy.

In the jeep, which was rigged up like a miniature bus, Joe sat with Beth, while Manny, after a moment, joined Reed in the front seat.

Joe told his story.

When he had finished, Beth said, "I'm proud of you, Joe. You did a very brave thing, you know, to go ahead right to the end—when you'd been warned you might be murdered."

"Joe did a brave thing." Manny sounded grudging as he gave praise that he obviously felt was expected of him.

"It was *Manny* who found *me*—maybe saved my life," Joe protested. The conversation was making him very uncomfortable. "Manny, I don't guess I really thanked you. I don't believe I would have gone after a guy if I was as sore at him as you were at me. Hadn't we better get back to Gouldings so that the search can be called off? The plane saw me and dropped a note, but will everybody else know?"

"Everybody knows already—the plane has a radio. Take it easy, Joe," Reed said.

Take it easy! Reed was a nice guy, but sometimes he didn't get the pitch. How could he feel like taking it easy? Did Reed think he could laugh off causing such an uproar? But that wasn't the main thing. Joe still had to persuade Manny not to act like a sorehead about his claim.

Manny seemed restless, as if he was going to get out of the jeep any minute and ride off. His horse still stood patiently, ground-tied near by.

"Mr. Reed," Joe asked, "could you drive us to wherever

Manny's pick-up is? He'll want it if he's going back to the claim—and I hope he is. I could ride back with him."

Joe would a lot rather drive with Beth, but there would be time to do that after he got this business with Manny settled. He hoped that his offer of practical help would remove one small excuse Manny might use to delay, or even to avoid, returning to the claim.

"I sold the pick-up as soon as I got to Kayenta. A pick-up is no good here. There's too much sand."

"Come along with us to Gouldings, then," Beth said warmly. "I'll drive you back to Shiprock in my car."

Manny said nothing. His eyes looked away from the others toward the Bear's Claw, which made a sharp gouge in the sky not far to the north.

"You should go back now," Manny finally broke his silence, "while you have light enough to see the way. I'm staying here. I am a Navaho."

Reed understood now, if he hadn't guessed already, that Manny had not been persuaded to do anything about his claim.

"Hosteen, why don't you do Joe a favor and talk this over a little more," Reed said earnestly. "Joe risked his life to do *you* a favor."

Manny subsided in the front seat with apparent reluctance.

"I think I know how you feel," Reed continued. "White men have done many terrible things to your people, and to you. I know how Navahos still talk about the old days when Kit Carson and his soldiers killed all your sheep and many of your men and even your women and children. When I first came to the Reservation, there were still old people who remembered how he drove the Navahos, like cattle, far away from your home, on what you call the Long Walk. I know that one of the leaders in those times was the great chief Manuelito. He fought bravely for your people. Are you named after him?"

"Maybe," was all Manny would say.

"Manuelito gave up fighting the whites when he saw he could not help his people by making war. Long ago I heard what Manuelito said when he was an old man. He was talking to a younger leader, and these are his exact words: 'My grandchild, the whites have many things which we Navahos need. But we cannot get them. It is as though the whites were in a grassy canyon and there they have wagons, plows, and plenty of food. We Navahos are up on the dry mesa. We can hear them talking but we cannot get to them. My grandchild, education is the ladder. Tell our people to take it.' "

Joe had never heard of the old chief Manuelito, but he felt sure Reed was ringing some bell in Manny's mind. If only Manny could somehow get the idea that he would be carrying on a Navaho tradition if he went back to his claim, instead of staying away from it.

"I've always remembered those words of Manuelito's," Reed went on, "and, Hosteen, I'm sure you do too. You have probably had more education than any young man in Monument Valley. You can help your people a great deal if you use it. Remember: 'The whites have many things which we Navahos need.' "

What Reed said was true. Manny would have to admit it, unless he closed his mind completely against the whites. And he hadn't been able to do that yet. He had gone down into the canyon to save Joe's life.

"And, Hosteen," Beth broke in, "you don't have to stop being a Navaho when you use things that come from a white man. Navahos have always been quick to borrow useful things and ideas from other people. That's one of the wonderful things about you. I've just been reading a book about it. I found out something you probably know already. The Spanish brought the first sheep into this country three or four hundred years ago. The very sheep you love came from white men—and so did your horses. It was just an accident that white men had them and you didn't. Before horses came, Navahos always had to walk anywhere they went. But you didn't stop being Navahos when you learned to herd sheep and ride horses."

This was an angle Joe had never dreamt of. It was news to him that the Indians hadn't always had sheep and horses. Maybe it would be news to Manny. Maybe it would give him the idea that he wouldn't be a traitor to his people if he did some new things, the way his ancestors had done.

"It seems to me," Beth went on, "you can still be a Navaho and drive a truck—or dig a uranium mine. I know very well that a lot of white people think you ought to become just like whites. But that doesn't mean you have to. And you certainly don't have to let white men keep all their good things for themselves."

Manny gave a quick glance at Beth as she said this, then his eyes went back in the distance toward the Bear's Claw.

Joe could see that her argument had made an impression.

"Oh, I wish you would go back to your claim," Beth said with such smiling, generous insistence that Joe couldn't see how any stubbornness could survive in Manny. "You could do such wonderful things for yourself and your people with the money you'd make. You could learn to be a pilot, and maybe have your own helicopter or plane. Joe told me he's sure you'd be a good pilot."

Beth was certainly smart. Joe knew the idea of owning a helicopter would appeal to Manny. He was fascinated with everything about the Canary. And anybody with half an eye could see that he wanted to learn to fly.

"Beth gives me an idea, Manny," Joe said. "You save your claim and get all the money you can out of it, and I'll teach you to fly. You'll be able to buy your own copter and fly it anywhere. Mr. Reed here's told me he thinks the Indian Service ought to use copters. You could set up an ambulance service, too—couldn't he, Beth?"

At last Manny spoke. Turning to Joe he said, "What are you going to do now?"

"I told you I would go back to your claim and help you make the improvements. After that I'll get a job."

"With Burns?"

"Not by a long sight! I wouldn't work for him, even if he wanted me to—which he doesn't, you can be sure of that. I'll probably have to go to California or someplace where they really use a lot of copters."

"Would you stay here—if you could fly a copter? Would you stay and teach me to fly?"

"Would I! I'd like to stay here the rest of my life."

Manny slowly opened the car door and walked over to his pony. Joe and Beth and Reed watched every move he made. Deliberately he unsaddled the horse and removed the bridle. Then he gave the horse a sharp slap on the rump and sent him trotting off in the direction of the Bear's Claw. Picking up the saddle and bridle, he threw them onto the floor of the jeep.

"I will go back to the claim."

Manny announced this, probably the greatest decision of

his life, in a voice that was very quiet, but he sounded so calm and sure that Joe was certain this impulsive act had something about it very different from his earlier decisions to leave Spencer's ranch and to abandon his claim.

Joe switched on the radio as he took the wheel to give Beth a rest. She had driven a long stretch after leaving Gouldings, where she and Joe and Manny spent the night. Reed had gone on in his car to Kayenta.

The radio announcer had already started with a round-up of the news. . . . "Two witnesses were cited for contempt of Congress today for refusal to answer questions regarding their political affiliations. . . ."

Beth turned it down. "Manny," she said, "last night you seemed unhappy because some of your people thought Joe was a witch. Did you hear what the radio said just now?"

Manny nodded and looked at her curiously.

"Well, there are white people who say that questioning witnesses like that is witch-hunting, too. Only we use new-fangled words like 'subversive' or 'communist-sympathizer.' But it's the same thing in the end. Navahos see that something bad has happened, and many of them believe a witch must have caused it. White people have troubles, too, and like as not they don't know what really causes them. Then somebody comes along and convinces them that if they get rid of 'subversives' or 'foreign agents' or whatever, everything will be all right. That starts a hunt. With us right now, it's a hunt for people who are trying to upset old beliefs, and we want to punish them, just the way Two Fingers was out to punish Joe for upsetting the good-luck pile. Don't think for one minute that there aren't some whites who believe in their own kind of witches."

"A lot of people don't agree with you about this subversive business, Beth," Joe said. "I'm not sure I do."

"I know," Beth said cheerfully. "But I bet I'm right." She turned the radio up.

". . . . A new series of tests of atomic weapons has been scheduled for. . . ."

"Do you mind?" Beth said and switched the radio off. She was silent for a minute, then turned to Manny. "Uranium from this beautiful, hungry, sick land of yours is going into bombs that can kill people."

"Don't I know!" Joe agreed with her now. "I saw Hiroshima once when I was on leave in Japan. We flattened the whole place with a bomb during the war. Killed thousands of people, I guess. Did you see it while you were over there, Manny?"

"Didn't see it, but I heard about it," Manny said.

Nobody said anything for a while as the car sped along over the bumpy road. Then Beth spoke again.

"We could do wonderful things in the hospital with some of the products that come from uranium, such as discovering disease and curing it. But so far not a gram of uranium has stayed on the Reservation to help the Navaho people. I certainly wish the tribe would get busy and find a way to keep its uranium and use it for the good of Navahos—and everybody."

The blasted land on either side of the road looked to Joe as if an atom bomb had struck and life was only beginning to return.

For a long time Joe and Beth and Manny were silent.

Beth spoke first. In her soft, low voice she said to Manny,

"Reed told me you drove out to Monument Valley with the pretty girl who danced with you at the squaw dance."

Manny looked at her cautiously, but said nothing.

"You've got to get used to girls like me, Manny. I don't mean any harm by prying into things that are none of my business. I'm just interested in people and I can't help asking questions. I want you to be happy. I guess you know what I mean. Are you? . . ." Beth's voice trailed off.

Manny thought a long time before replying, then he said, "Our uncles are going to talk about it. I guess now I will be able to make a big present with the money from the mine."

"I'm so glad for you," Beth said earnestly. "I could just tell Dezbah was a nice girl."

Joe was left partly in the dark by this exchange, and Beth sensed it. "Manny and Dezbah want to get married—isn't that splendid?" she said. "A brother of Manny's mother and a brother of Dezbah's mother are arranging it. That's the way Navahos do it. And the groom always brings a gift for his bride's family when he comes to live with the bride. Will you go back and live with Dezbah in Monument Valley?"

"Dezbah wants to live wherever it is best to live," Manny replied.

"You're lucky to have a girl like that—one who doesn't feel she has to live in a hogan next to her mother's. This way you'll both be able to do what you want to do."

Manny was embarrassed. He looked out the window on his side of the car. He stared at the walking beam of a pump out in the sagebrush that was steadily lifting oil from deep in the earth up to the surface. And nearby a small boy on horseback was following a flock of sheep in search of grass. . . .

Ahead now was the green blur of trees around the hospital

at Shiprock—and closer was the outline of the new uranium reduction plant. That was where the ore from Manny's claim would go. But Joe's earlier uranium-fever dreams did not return. A firm decision was in their place.

He was a copter pilot in a land that could sure use copters. Somehow he'd find a way to fly here—in a copter that had a supercharger. And he'd teach Manny to fly—and Beth.

He and Beth would take the first flight, and from high—really high—in the air he'd look down on this new homeland of his. From such a height he was sure he would see what he sought—the way things fitted together.

No, "fit" was too quiet and orderly a word in this country of ever-changing, ever-extreme contrasts. But even down here on the road approaching Shiprock, the whole world seemed to make better sense than it ever had before. And it was an exciting place in which to live.

About the Author Born in Boulder, Colorado, of pioneer stock, Franklin Folsom is a graduate of the University of Colorado and, as a Rhodes Scholar, studied English literature at Oxford. He worked, among other jobs, as mountain guide, a library assistant, a book-reviewer, an instructor at Swarthmore College, an able-bodied seaman, and a journalist. Currently he devotes his full time to writing books for young people.

Now he lives in Roosevelt, New Jersey, with his wife and two children. In his spare time Mr. Folsom camps out, explores caves, and has become an active, though amateur archeologist. An enthusiast for the American West, he says, "My boyhood, when I learned authentic Indian dances from Ralph Hubbard, and my present interests have come to sharp focus on the Navaho Reservation, when the past and present of Indian life have their most dramatic meeting point." *Search in the Desert* reflects his knowledge of the Navaho country gained through long summers camping in the Navaho Reservation.